Molly
And The
Railroad Tycoon

STEPHEN OVERHOLSER

Thorndike Press • **Chivers Press**
Thorndike, Maine USA **Bath, England**

This Large Print edition is published by Thorndike Press, USA and by Chivers Press, England.

Published in 2001 in the U.S. by arrangement with Golden West Literary Agency.

Published in 2001 in the U.K. by arrangement with Golden West Literary Agency.

U.S. Hardcover 0-7862-3240-4 (Western Series Edition)
U.K. Hardcover 0-7540-4529-3 (Chivers Large Print)
U.K. Softcover 0-7540-4530-7 (Camden Large Print)

The text of this Large Print edition is unabridged.
Other aspects of the book may vary from the original edition.

Set in 16 pt. Plantin by Minnie B. Raven.

Printed in the United States on permanent paper.

British Library Cataloguing-in-Publication Data available

Library of Congress Cataloging-in-Publication Data

Overholser, Stephen.
    Molly and the railroad tycoon / Stephen Overholser.
      p. cm.
    "A new heroine from the old West."
    ISBN 0-7862-3240-4 (lg. print : hc : alk. paper)
    1. Owens, Molly (Fictitious character) —Fiction.
  2. Women private investigators — Montana — Fiction.
  3. Railroads — Fiction. 4. Montana — Fiction.
  5. Large type books.
  I. Title.
PS3565.V43 M57 2001
  813′.54—dc21   00-054465

MOLLY
AND THE
RAILROAD TYCOON

MOLLY
AND THE
RAILROAD TYCOON

CHAPTER I

The land was fattened by snow. From horseback Molly saw the white expanse of eastern Montana under a dark and threatening sky, an enormous snowfield softly obscuring hills and valleys and ravines. From horizon to horizon the white land was undisturbed for all but one long, straight line.

The rails of the North American & Pacific ran east and west as far as Molly could see. The steel tracks that seemed to come together at a point far ahead were paralleled by the bare poles of a telegraph line. Four or five miles back that line had been cut.

Molly turned in the saddle and saw Newman coming. A dumpy, pale man wearing a mackinaw and a heavy wool cap with the earflaps tied under his fleshy chin, he made a strange sight. Since discovering the downed line he had clenched a revolver in one hand and his field glasses in the other, often riding through this white, silent land with the glasses pressed to his eyes.

Like Molly, Oliver Newman was a Fenton operative who had been rushed here from Denver. Outlaws had stopped three NA&P trains in the last four weeks, and the rail line's owner, Preston Brooks, had had enough. In addition to putting armed guards on every train, he had brought in a dozen operatives from the Fenton Investigative Agency to ride the tracks.

But unlike Molly, Oliver Newman was not accustomed to field work. Investigating businesses and conducting midnight audits were his specialty. Now after a day on horseback in the Montana cold he was so chilled and saddlesore that a perpetual grimace lined his face.

Molly approached high snowbanks from a drift that had been plowed out by a steam engine and drew rein until her partner caught up. Newman had lowered his field glasses and opened his mouth to speak when a dark, round hole appeared in his forehead. Head snapping back, he fell out of the saddle as the winter silence was shattered by a rifle shot. Molly saw him sink into the snow, mouth still open.

She wheeled her horse around, but before she could put spurs to the frightened animal, a second shot drove her into the air. The next thing she knew she lay sprawled in the snow, unable to breathe.

Pain spread through her chest.

"Two dead detectives! Didja see that big one drop? Got him square in the head!"

Molly tried to turn toward the high-pitched, squeaky voice but could not move. She stared straight up at the leaden sky.

Movement caught her eye, and at the edge of her vision she saw two men rise up behind the far snowbank. They brushed snow from the fronts of their long sheep-skin coats. Again the squeaky voice carried to her across the wintry silence.

"Maybe they're carrying money. . . ."

Molly gasped as the two gunmen came down the slope of the snowbank toward the tracks. Her pained lungs filled with cold air, and she exhaled a great cloud.

"By damn, that one's still alive!"

Molly turned her head, gasping again. Through the cloud of her own breath she saw the squeaky-voiced man jack a round into his Winchester. He was a long-faced, bug-eyed man, a head shorter than the outlaw at his side. As though living a night-mare, she saw him thrust the weapon to his shoulder.

Molly stared as the gun was leveled at her. The bug-eyed man squinted over the sights. She saw the blast and her ears rang with its roar. Snow sprayed into her face.

Cheeks stinging, she brought a hand to her chest. She fumbled for her coat buttons, desperately trying to reach inside for the Colt .38 in her shoulder holster.

"Missed him!" The bug-eyed outlaw swore and levered another round into the rifle chamber.

"Hold it! Listen!"

Molly heard drumming sounds in the distance. The sounds grew louder, the hooves of galloping horses striking the frozen earth like hammers.

"Damn! Country's crawling with Fentons!"

The pair of outlaws whirled and ran back up the side of the snowbank, their boots plunging deeply into it. They hurdled over the top, and moments later Molly heard the soft sounds of horses running in the snow.

She wanted to get up and give pursuit, but her body did not obey her mind. She lay in the snow beside the tracks, paralyzing pain rippling through her chest. A wave of heat surged through her. As the sounds of running horses became louder, her face broke out in a sweat.

Next she heard the surprised and angry curses of men who have come upon death. She closed her eyes.

★ ★ ★

Molly awoke in what she thought was a mansion in motion. *Impossible,* she thought, as she lay in a soft and warm bed and looked up at a ceiling of polished walnut. Yet this place was moving. She turned her head. The richly grained dark wood lined the walls, too, where cut-glass lamps were mounted on gleaming brass brackets. Windows were covered by heavy curtains of a deep maroon color. Hearing the steady clicking of wheels over rails, she realized she lay inside a custom-built railroad coach.

She tried to raise up on an elbow, but the effort brought a cry of pain. And with the blast of pain through her chest came the vivid memory of the squeaky-voiced outlaw leveling his big Winchester at her, squinting . . . aiming . . . pulling the trigger. That memory was like her worst nightmare come true, deeply etched into her mind and her dreams.

Reaching under the covers, Molly unbuttoned her blouse and gingerly felt for a bandage. To her amazement she did not find one. The soreness was there, all right, but no wound. She raised her head up and looked, seeing no bullet hole in her blouse. For a long moment she could not sort out

11

the real from the unreal. She had been shot, yet there was no bullet wound.

Light spilled into the room when a door at the end of the coach swung open. Molly pulled up the blanket to cover herself, and turned her head far enough to see a broad-shouldered man come in.

"You're awake," he said.

Molly watched as he came around the bed and stopped beside her. He was a handsome man with wide-set cheekbones, square jaw, and a full mustache. His eyebrows arched over his dark eyes in a way that gave power to his gaze.

"You slept hard, like you were never going to wake up," he said. "I know. I was here all night." He jerked his head toward a leather upholstered chair in a corner of the coach.

Molly's mouth was dry, and she had to swallow before she could speak. "What . . . happened?"

"You were shot out of the saddle," he said, "and left for dead."

"I know, but —"

The man turned away and went to a small table beside the high-backed chair. "Your life was saved by Mister Colt," he said, coming back to the bed. "And by your fellow operatives who brought you here."

Molly saw that he had picked up her Colt Lightning Model .38. The frame behind the cylinder was scored and bent.

"Damnedest thing I ever saw," he said. "When those Fentons carried you in, I saw the hole in your coat and thought you were dead. Those men did, too. Your partner didn't make it. Then I pulled away your coat and saw this revolver."

He gazed down at her for a moment. "Look, I'm glad you're alive, but I'm damned angry with Horace Fenton for sending a woman out on a job like this. I asked for his best operatives from Denver and Chicago — good gunhands. Don't worry, he'll hear about this from me."

"You're Preston Brooks?" Molly asked.

He nodded. "I'm, uh, sorry I didn't introduce myself. I'm a bit upset about this whole thing."

The apology did not come easily. Molly sensed he was a man unaccustomed to apologizing or explaining his actions to anyone.

"Mr. Brooks," she said, "I assure you that I am as well qualified for this job as any operative in the Fenton agency." She held his gaze and added, "Man or woman."

He looked down at her skeptically.

"Truth is, Miss Owens, I didn't even know any Fentons were women." He shook his head. "No, this is no task for a lady. You may be good at trailing wandering husbands or wives in Denver, but there is greater danger here than you'll find in some domestic spat."

Molly felt her face grow warm. "I've been faced with danger before, Mr. Brooks. If you'd care to look at my record with the Fenton agency —"

"That won't be necessary, Miss Owens," he said.

Molly realized she wasn't getting through to him, and decided that it was difficult to argue persuasively when she was flat on her back. She changed the subject.

"Were those two outlaws captured?" she asked.

Brooks shook his head again. "At nightfall your friends lost them."

Molly clenched her teeth and raised up on her right elbow. "I'll take up the trail."

"No, you won't," Brooks said.

Molly stared at him, her anger rising.

"You're in no shape to ride," Brooks said, moving away from the bed to the door. "I'm taking you to the Union Pacific spur, and from there you'll return to

Denver by way of Cheyenne — along with the body of your partner."

Molly watched him open the door and leave the coach, then sank back to the pillow. She was angry and frustrated, yet at the same time knew he was right. The bruise on her side was severe. She touched it gingerly, wondering if any ribs were cracked.

Admitting defeat came hard. More than anything she wanted to ride down that squeaky-voiced, bug-eyed outlaw. She wanted to bring that one in herself, disarmed and handcuffed, and put that nightmare to rest.

CHAPTER II

"I don't know, Molly. I just don't know why you do it."

With an expression of exasperation and worry on her face, Mrs. Boatwright stood at the foot of Molly's bed, arms folded across her thick body. "Every time you leave here, I wonder if I'll ever see you again. And every time I do see you, I wonder how bad you're hurt. Chewed by a grizzly bear, shot — what's next?"

Buck, a green-eyed, red-haired boy of fourteen, sat on the end of the bed, grinning at Molly with open admiration. In response to Molly's telegraphed message from Cheyenne, he had driven Mrs. Boatwright's carriage to Denver's Union Station and met her train.

"You need me to go along with you," Buck said. "I'll protect you, like I done when I scared that bear off."

" 'Did,' " Mrs. Boatwright said.

"That's right, I did," he said, glancing at her.

Molly smiled at them. "I'm home safe and sound. That's what counts."

"You're home safe this time," Mrs. Boatwright said, "but I know you. The minute you start feeling good, you'll get restless. And before long you'll go looking for trouble."

"I don't look for it," Molly said. "Trouble has a way of finding me."

"That's because you get right smack in the way of it," Mrs. Boatwright said. "If you'd get married and start a home life, you wouldn't get yourself chewed and bruised."

"Chewed and bruised," Buck repeated, laughing. "Chewed and bruised."

"Listen, you two," Molly said, "I'm supposed to be getting some rest. You heard Doc Whittaker say there wasn't anything wrong with me that a couple days' rest won't cure —"

"Three weeks' rest," Mrs. Boatwright interrupted. "I heard him say that. And I heard him say you've got two broken ribs."

"Well, when is my resting time going to start?" Molly asked.

"Buck, I believe she's trying to get rid of us," Mrs. Boatwright said. She turned and went to the door.

The boy stood. "I want to hear all about your ride in the Silver Comet. Do you know that Preston Brooks has the fastest steam engine in the world? He's had it going 100 miles an hour —"

"Buck," Mrs. Boatwright said.

Molly winked at him. "We'll talk about it later." She watched him walk across the bedroom to the door. Mrs. Boatwright followed him out and closed the door behind them.

Molly leaned her head back on the pillow, becoming aware of the pain in her side as she took a deep breath.

If you'd get married and start a home life. . . . Mrs. Boatwright's words echoed in Molly's mind. She took another deep breath and winced.

I'm not married, she thought, *because I've never met the right man.* How many times had she tossed off that reply to the nosey spinsters and widows who lived in Mrs. Boatwright's Boarding House for Ladies? Too many times to count, and she had thought it even more times.

The right man. In a way she had met him. He was made up of facets of several men in her life. In part, he was a confidence man named Charley Castle. Charley had excited her and inspired her imagination. He had been a wonderful, impulsive lover who had had a way of appearing when she least expected him. But he'd been a tumble-weed, a liar by profession, and not the marrying kind. Now he was dead, gunned down by a trigger-happy posse who'd cornered the wrong man.

The right man. In Cripple Creek she had met a young attorney, a man she admired for his strong will. But that very trait had divided them, and when all was said and done they had come out on opposite sides. Her side won, and she lost him.

The right man. Molly had fallen in love with Cole Estes. Even though he was a notorious outlaw and had spent much of his life on the run, he was not of the cruel breed Molly had run into in eastern Montana. Cole Estes was like a general. His objective was to relieve large banks and Union Pacific express cars of their cash. The opposing army was made up of U.S. marshals and various hired thugs and bounty hunters. Cole Estes had frequently defeated the enemy, but he lost the war, and Molly had watched a good and strong man ride into Mexico.

The right man.

Molly had never met him, but she had caught glimpses of him. One day she would find him. Then — and only then — would she be content to leave behind her hard-earned career and meet new challenges with a good man at her side.

So she told herself. But the next day her mood abruptly changed. Under a barrage of protests from Mrs. Boatwright, she left her bed and went to the funeral of Oliver Newman. No one else came.

As she sat in the empty and eerie funeral parlor, she stared at the pine casket and wondered if all the Fentons and Pinkertons and operatives of other investigative agencies came to the same end — without family or friends. She herself had no family left, and sitting in this cold, silent parlor made her think of her own funeral.

Molly walked out into the light of day, feeling weighted by her own mortality. And she could not rid her mind of Mrs. Boatwright's words.

Maybe it was time she gave up this dangerous profession. Maybe it was time to find the nearest healthy man and settle for him, raise a houseful of pink-cheeked boys and girls, watch them grow up, and live out her years in peace.

That was what a woman was supposed to do. Mrs. Boatwright had reminded her of it often enough, saying that a woman must marry "before the bloom is off the rose."

Nonsense, Molly had argued. She would know when the time was right.

But Mrs. Boatwright was relentless. "You young women don't know the loneliness old age brings," she said ominously.

Even though Molly steadfastly disagreed with her on this point, she still admired the woman. Mrs. Boatwright had married young, but had never borne children. Her husband had been a mining engineer who had made a fortune in Leadville and in triumph had come to Denver, where he built his mansion in the Capitol Hill section of town. He enjoyed his riches, traveling to Europe several times and investing in other mining ventures.

Upon his sudden death at age 54, Mrs. Boatwright did not inherit the Boatwright fortune. She inherited the Boatwright debt. Through bad investments the fortune was gone, and her husband had borrowed to the hilt.

With no knowledge of business or finances, Mrs. Boatwright had argued and cajoled until the family banker agreed to postpone the sale of the great mansion. She'd had an idea. She would use her talent and long experience as a homemaker and convert her elegant home into a residence for ladies of means.

The scheme worked. Within two years Mrs. Boatwright had quadrupled her monthly payments to the bank. And the women who lived in her house, young and old, became her family. Now Buck was added to the fold, brought here by Molly. He was the son of Cole Estes, headed for trouble until Molly intervened.

Molly returned to her room on the second floor of the Boatwright mansion. The day passed darkly under a stormy sky. After a night of fitful sleep she awoke to the sight of a sky filled with large snow-flakes. They floated to the ground like torn tissue.

The snow continued through the morning, but at noon the sun broke through, surprisingly warm. The snow began to melt, and by late afternoon it was gone. When Mrs. Boatwright brought Molly's dinner on a tray, she happily announced the arrival of spring — crocuses had broken through the damp earth on the south side of the mansion.

Molly smiled with her. Yet she was not cheered.

By the beginning of the third week of her convalescence, after another brief but furious snowstorm — the last gasp of winter — the pain in Molly's side had become a dull ache. On the mend and feeling much better, Molly still did not leave her room except to go downstairs for meals with the ladies or into the solarium to sun herself and read.

The glassed solarium on the mansion's south side gave a panoramic view of the Rocky Mountains. High peaks and foothills were pure white against a blue sky, but outside the windows all the snow had melted, and the warm, bright days turned the grass pale green.

Every sunny morning now sparrows sang as they flew about the sculpted hedges outside, and robins puffed their chests while they hopped in the grass in pursuit of early worms. Mrs. Boatwright shrieked with delight when the first crocus spread its red flower to the sun. Doors and windows were opened during the warm hours of midday, and Molly caught the beckoning scent of moist soil and new growth.

But the good sounds and sights of the new season did not brighten her dark mood. That did not happen until an unexpected visitor came to the mansion, insisting loudly upon seeing Molly.

The commotion brought her downstairs. She stepped into the front parlor to find Mrs. Boatwright, hands on her plump hips, confronting Preston Brooks.

CHAPTER III

"Mr. Brooks," Molly said in surprise.

Mrs. Boatwright dropped her hands from her hips and turned around. "You know this . . . gentleman?"

"Yes, I do," Molly said, stepping into the carpeted parlor. She saw that Preston Brooks' square jaw was set in anger.

"Well, all right then," Mrs. Boatwright said reluctantly. She gave him a final glare before leaving the room.

Preston Brooks came a step closer to Molly, his stylish felt hat in hand. He wore a camel's hair overcoat over a dark blue suit. "I seem to have gotten off on the wrong foot with your landlady."

"Mrs. Boatwright is protective," Molly said, smiling. She gestured around the room. "This is her home, and she treats all of us who live here as family."

"A mother hen, if you ask me," he said. "She seemed to want a full accounting from me before letting me past the door."

"Let me take your coat and hat, Mr. Brooks," Molly said, holding out her hand, "and we'll go into the solarium — where you can give me a full accounting."

Despite himself, Brooks grinned. He shouldered out of his overcoat. "Well, at least you didn't lose your sense of humor in Montana."

By the solarium windows, where sunlight streamed into the room and spilled across the terra-cotta tiled floor and the potted palms, they sat facing one another in deeply cushioned wicker chairs. For several moments neither spoke. Under his crisply tailored suit, Brooks wore a white shirt and silk tie with a gold pin. With his full mustache neatly trimmed and his sandy hair combed straight back from his broad forehead, he was as handsome and distinguished as Molly remembered him.

He was not a man for small talk, she sensed, and he either spoke directly to the point, or was silent until he thought of a way to get there. Right now he was thinking.

"The last I heard," Molly said, "the outlaws who ambushed Oliver Newman and me were never caught."

"That's right," Brooks said. "But with a show of force, I managed to drive them into hiding." He paused, and then said bluntly, "I've come here to hire you, Miss Owens — if you will consent to work for me."

Molly was surprised, not only by the request, but by his almost apologetic manner of asking her.

"You may not know it," he went on, "but your employer, Horace Fenton, is a long-time friend of mine. When I complained that he had sent a woman to do a man's job, Horace promptly came to Chicago and personally told me of your record with the agency. I now realize I was mistaken about you, quite mistaken. You are a beautiful woman, very ladylike, and I thought, well, I thought you were completely out of your element."

Brooks exhaled, turning his hands palms up. "Miss Owens, I made an ass out of myself, pure and simple. You are a top-notch investigator, undoubtedly one of the best in the country."

Molly smiled. "I doubt that I can live up to that reputation." She added, "You weren't entirely wrong to take me off the investigation. I was in no shape to continue the pursuit."

"Were you badly injured?" he asked.

"Just a bruise," Molly replied, "a deep one where my revolver struck my ribs. I'm as good as new now." Having stretched the truth a bit, she asked, "Just what sort of assignment do you have in mind, Mr. Brooks?"

"My friends call me Pres," he said. "I'd like to count you as one."

She smiled. "I'm Molly."

"All right, Molly," he said with enthusiasm, "let me give you the background of this thing. Plenty of people told me I'd never run steel through Montana. First, I was told I couldn't get title to the land I'd need. Well, after I bought and swapped for a right-of-way from one end of the state to the other, I was told the weather would stop me. The winters were too severe. Then after I laid steel people told me there wasn't enough business in the whole state of Montana to support a railroad."

Brooks paused. "The world is full of skeptics, Molly, full of people with big mouths and small ideas. I built my railroad, not just in Montana but in Washington, too, and now I have the only northern route between Chicago and Puget Sound. Think of what that means."

"Shipping," Molly said.

"That's right," he said. "I'll be transporting American goods and passengers to the coast, and bringing back foreign goods." He leaned forward in his chair. "But that's only part of my plan. The North American & Pacific is my irrigation ditch, and I'm going to use it to flood

Montana with people. For the last year I've advertised in every state in the Union and every country in Europe. I'm selling land for a fraction of what it's worth and providing free transportation to folks looking for a new start in life. That's what they'll find in Montana. Dry farming in that north country is the wave of the future, and I aim to teach hundreds of folks how to prosper behind the plow."

"Farming without irrigation?" Molly asked.

Brooks nodded, looking at her intently. "I've already proved it can be done. Wheat grows shoulder high up there. If my plan works, all of eastern Montana will be a golden wheat field one day. It's just a matter of bringing folks in and showing them how."

"But there must be a problem," Molly said, "or you wouldn't be sitting here right now."

"I've had problems," he said. "NA&P rolling stock has been damaged, homestead locator offices have been looted and my men beaten, and you know about the outlaws. These are separate incidents, but I believe they come from one source. You see, my offer of land to farmers is not popular with the cattle interests in Montana."

28

"And you think they want to put you out of business?" Molly asked.

"Not out of business," he said. "They depend on the NA&P to ship their cattle. No, I think they want to scare off the farmers. The cattlemen have always had that range land to themselves, and they want to keep it that way."

"Are the cattlemen organized against you?" Molly asked.

"That's the big question," Brooks said. "None of them like what I'm doing, but how many of them would condone what has happened, or harbor known outlaws, is another question. It's one I want you to answer, if you'll take on this job."

They regarded one another for a long moment. Molly had heard the intensity in his voice as he described his grand plan. He was driven to fulfill a vision, a man of powerful presence, and Molly had been stirred by him.

"After talking to Horace Fenton," Brooks went on, "I'm convinced you're the right operative for this investigation." He added, "You'll need to work undercover, of course."

Molly nodded. "I have an idea for a ruse that will allow me to roam freely without raising suspicion."

"Good," he said. "Horace told me you're highly trained — that you can ride and shoot and are skilled in cracking safes and picking door locks. Is that true?"

"Yes," Molly said.

"And you have mastered some sort of hand-to-hand combat technique in your training back in New York," he said, eyebrows arched as he studied her.

"A kindly Japanese man taught me how to defend myself," Molly said, "in case I meet someone who is rude."

Brooks laughed heartily. "I'll mind my manners." He asked, "You'll take the case?"

"Yes," Molly said, feeling a tingle of excitement deep inside. Cooped up too long, this was the challenge she needed. She stood and held out her hand.

Preston Brooks fairly leaped to his feet. He grasped her hand and gave it a vigorous shake.

CHAPTER IV

Wolf Ridge, Montana, had been a ramshackle cow town of log cabins and weathered lean-tos until the completion of the North American & Pacific Railroad. With rail traffic from Chicago to the West Coast, Wolf Ridge had quickly become the major supply center and shipping point for the cattle ranches of eastern Montana.

Now the town boasted a new main street with a large hotel, The Montanan, and false-fronted stores and small office buildings. On the west side of town was the saloon district. On the other side of Main Street stood new houses, a red brick schoolhouse, two churches, and a whitewashed frame auditorium with a sign over the front double doors: "Wolf Ridge Community Hall."

As Molly stepped down from the NA&P passenger coach, she looked past the steeproofed depot down the length of Main Street. Between the boardwalks an early spring thaw had left soupy puddles in the rutted street, making an obstacle course for a fat woman who lifted her dress as she crossed.

Molly slung her handbag over her shoulder and carried her valise to the far edge of the loading platform. The fat woman had slogged out of deep mud and stepped up to the boardwalk. She stomped her feet there and walked to a doorway under a sign painted with a star: "County Sheriff."

Molly headed down there, too. She had walked a short distance on the boardwalk when she heard three blasts of the steam engine's whistle. She glanced back to see the engineer, a man with a walrus mustache and wearing a greasy cap and overalls, lean out of the cab while a switchman waved. The engineer pulled the train onto a siding. Some of the freight cars would be left behind for unloading, and empty box cars would be picked up.

Molly passed by the plate-glass windows of Geary's Hardware & Ranch Supply and a millinery next door and went on to the doorway of the sheriff's office. Through the window she saw the fat woman talking to a bald man who matched Preston Brooks' description of Sheriff Willard Jenkins.

As Molly opened the door and stepped inside, she realized the discussion between the sheriff and the fat woman was not a friendly one.

"There's my damned fine, paid in full," the fat woman said, slapping a pair of twenty-dollar gold pieces on the desk that separated them. "Only I think you ought to have the decency to wear a mask like any other bandit."

"I told you, Lillie," he said, "this whole deal was a compromise. The city council —"

"Nobody asked *me* if I wanted to compromise," she interrupted. "Nobody asked me nothing, but by god I have to pay or get run out of town."

"Now, Lillie, nobody's going to run you out —"

"Those do-gooders on the council want me out of Wolf Ridge, don't tell me they don't," Lillie said. "Their wives are all in the Decency League, and they'd like nothing better than to tear my house down a board at a time."

If the fat woman was aware of Molly's presence, she gave no sign. Taking a deep breath, she launched into another tirade. "Do-gooders, Willard. If you let them run me out, who's next? They're against everything — dancing, drinking, card playing, women —"

Now the lawman nodded in Molly's direction. The fat woman turned around. gave Molly the once-over.

33

"You ever need work, girlie," she said, "come to my place. Pay's good, and I've got the best chef in Montana in my kitchen." With a last glance at the sheriff, she swept past Molly to the door. She went out, slamming it behind her.

The sheriff winced. Molly smiled and asked, "She operates a brothel?"

He nodded. "Don't take offense at Lillie, ma'am. She's mad at the whole town right now, maybe the whole world."

"I'm not a do-gooder, sheriff," Molly said, "or a do-badder."

Jenkins grinned, showing missing front teeth under a scarred lip. In his day, Molly thought as she looked at the man, he'd been a tough hand behind the badge.

"Lillie's right," Sheriff Jenkins said. "She's been in business here since Wolf Ridge was nothing but a collection of cabins, and now all the *good* folks of town want her to leave. Last night the town fathers burned the midnight oil to come up with this new ordinance: Prostitution is illegal, punishable by a $40 fine." He added with chagrin, "The fine is to be collected at the end of every month."

Molly chuckled. "That's a tax, sheriff."

"The councilmen call it a fine," he said. "They figure everybody will be satisfied now that the law is being enforced. But I've got a feeling everybody's going to be dissatisfied."

"Where does that leave you, sheriff?" Molly asked.

"Right slap in the middle," he replied. He looked at her. "Here I am, rattling on to you without even finding out what your business is. What can I do for you, ma'am?"

Molly set her valise down and reached into her handbag. She took out a photographic portrait of a round-cheeked man in his late twenties, clean shaven and well dressed.

"My name is Molly Owens, sheriff," she said, handing the portrait to him. "Have you seen this man?"

Jenkins held it at arm's length while tilting his head back. "No, I can't say that I have. Who is he?"

"My husband," Molly said. "I'm trying to find him."

"Oh, I see," he said. He handed the photograph back to her with a knowing look in his eyes. "Where are you from?"

"Chicago," Molly said. "I just got off the train. My husband . . ."

"Left you?" Jenkins said when she paused.

Molly nodded once.

"Look, ma'am," he said, "plenty of men come through Wolf Ridge nowadays, on the dodge or hunting work. Most of them stay a spell, and then hop a freight and move on. My advice is to let this feller go. Any man foolish enough to leave a fine-looking woman like yourself isn't good enough for you. Let him go. I know it sounds harsh. But you're young. You can make a new start."

Molly shook her head. "I can't turn back, not until I've searched for him. I want to find him — or find out what happened to him."

"I understand," Jenkins said. "Your pride is hurt, and folks back home are talking about you, aren't they? Other women have come to me with the same story. I'm sorry to have to tell you, but the truth is, I can't help you."

"Well, I'll stay in Wolf Ridge a few days," Molly said. "Maybe I can find someone who's seen him."

The lawman shrugged. "I can't stop you, ma'am. But I'd better warn you. There's a rough element in this town, and a woman wandering around by herself isn't safe."

"I'll be careful, sheriff," Molly said.

"See that you are," he said. "Especially after dark."

Molly left the county sheriff's office and stepped out to the edge of the boardwalk. The photograph she had brought was a studio portrait of Oliver Newman that she had found among his effects. Showing it to strangers here involved a certain risk if she stumbled onto Newman's killer and the face in the photograph was recognized. But she had decided the risk was worth taking. She wanted that murderer and his partner. If she had to force an outlaw's hand to do it, she was willing.

Directly across the street was The Montanan, a two-story hotel that had been financed by Preston Brooks. White, with red sashes at the windows, it was one of the few freshly painted buildings in a row that included a dry goods store, a barber shop, a combination funeral parlor and carpentry shop, and a small cafe that advertised "Home Cooked Meals."

Molly watched a pair of freight wagons pass by, their iron-tired wheels sloshing through mud. Both were pulled by matched draft horses, big muscular Percherons. Molly noticed the Bar S Bar brand on the animals.

The Bar S Bar was a huge cattle ranch owned by Sam Streeter. He was the most vocal of Preston Brooks' critics. Molly saw the loaded wagons roll through the sloppy street toward open range on the far side of town. Their hooves as big as platters, the horses tossed up great dollops of shiny mud.

She turned her attention back to the street in front of her. Puddles of liquid mud were connected by narrow canals left by wagon wheels. She gingerly stepped down, lifting her long skirt with her free hand. Her high button shoe sank into the mud past her ankle.

Holding her valise in one hand and her skirt in the other, she started across the soupy street. At the approach of a buggy she hurried and nearly lost her balance when her foot plunged to the bottom of a puddle. Teetering precariously, she heard a burst of laughter.

Molly took a long step forward to catch herself. Standing spread-legged in the mud, she looked up at the boardwalk in front of the hotel.

"Lady," said the man standing there with his hands on his hips, "you are some sight." He wore a wide-brimmed hat with a round crown, leather vest, and pinstriped trousers tucked into his boots. "You one of Lillie's new girls? I saw you with her in Jenkins' office."

The man came off the boardwalk and slogged through the mud toward her. "Give me that bag before you fall in and drown," he said, laughing again. "You won't be any good for a man if you're covered with mud. Here, grab aholt of my arm."

"I don't need your help," Molly said. She drew her feet together and straightened up.

"Sure, you do," he said, reaching down to grasp the handle of the valise.

Molly held on to it. "Leave me alone."

His cocky grin faded. "Look, lady, I didn't ruin the shine on my boots to be turned away — not by a woman like you. I'm taking your bag, and then I'll haul you over to Lillie's place and tell her to teach you some manners."

As he yanked the valise, Molly used a principle of jujitsu. She first resisted, and suddenly yielded. This move had the effect of propelling him backward, carried by his own momentum.

His eyes widened with amazement as his weight and strength were so quickly used against him. To avoid falling flat on his back, he half turned and dropped to one knee, releasing the handle of the valise. His other hand plunged into a puddle up to his elbow.

"Damn you, bitch!" he said.

Molly moved around him and went on to the boardwalk. She stepped up on it and went into The Montanan without looking back.

CHAPTER V

Molly checked into The Montanan. She was shown to a room on the second floor by the desk clerk, who carried her valise upstairs.

Furnished with a shiny brass bed, a dresser, and a wash stand with a basin and pitcher of water, the room smelled of cut lumber and wallpaper paste. When Preston Brooks had suggested she stay here, he'd said that workers had only recently finished the interior, and he'd showed her a flyer advertising The Montanan as the finest hotel between Chicago and Puget Sound. *Ever the promoter,* Molly had thought, even though she'd felt caught up in his enthusiasm.

The window overlooked Wolf Ridge's main street. As Molly pulled the gauze curtain aside she saw a group of cowhands on horseback splash by, their boots and leather chaps splattered with mud. On the boardwalk across the street a trio of fashionably dressed women walked past the sheriff's office. They entered the millinery next door.

Molly released the curtain and turned away from the window. She had not seen the man she had met in the middle of the street.

Molly pulled off her mud-caked shoes. She stood and unbuttoned her blue serge traveling dress. After stepping out of it, she slipped off her underclothes. She unbuckled the .22 two-shot derringer strapped to her thigh and tossed the weapon on the bed.

Her figure was trim and firm with a slim waist above the swell of her hips. Her large, pear-shaped breasts swung delicately as she moved to the wash stand and dipped a hand cloth into cool water in the basin.

Molly washed, rinsing soot and cinders from the train ride that had begun day before yesterday in Denver. Wolf Ridge was the logical starting point for her investigation, Preston Brooks had told her. This town was in the hub of the big cattle ranches in eastern Montana.

Her plan was to familiarize herself with the town and get her bearings. Then she would ride out to the surrounding ranches, and under the ruse of a wife searching for her runaway husband she would try to find out if any of the ranchmen were harboring train robbers.

Molly walked around town late that afternoon, following the boardwalks off Main Street to the saloon district. The buildings ranged from dilapidated drinking dens to gaily painted gambling and dance halls. At the end of the row Molly saw a two-story Victorian house where a lamp with a red chimney marked the front entrance.

The other side of town, as Molly had observed from the loading platform of the railroad depot, was the newest residential section. Fine houses lined the avenues here, along with the schoolhouse, the two churches, and the whitewashed community hall.

A playbill tacked to the door of the Wolf Ridge Community Hall caught Molly's eye. She moved closer and read the advertisement for a "Temperance Drama of Heartbreak & Despair, taken from the annals of True Life, presented by the Wolf Ridge Chapter of the Montana Decency League." In the starring role was Mrs. Helene Streeter. Molly read through the list of names in the cast, noticing the bottom one was "our honorable mayor, Mr. Alfred J. Wolcott."

Molly looked at the dates of the production, and saw that it had played last week. Next week a traveling entertainer was booked, a whistler who was renowned for his "amazing abilities in classical music and imitations of birds of the world."

Molly returned to the hotel and after an early supper she retired to her room. She lay in bed, glad to be away from the monotonous sounds of railcar wheels clicking over the tracks and the constant swaying and jerking of a passenger coach. She quickly fell asleep. She awoke, rested, before dawn.

At the first light of day she rode out of town on a rented saddle horse. The sleepy-eyed liveryman had given her directions to the headquarters of the Bar S Bar Ranch, pointing toward Main Street while describing a fork in the road she would find several miles out.

Knowing today's ride would be a long one, Molly had bought a box lunch in the hotel dining room, and now she carried it behind the saddle with her handbag. In that handbag were the tools of her trade — a set of lock probes, a ring of master skeleton keys, and extra rounds of ammunition. Her light jacket concealed a shoulder holster, where she carried a new Colt Lightning Model .38 revolver. Easily concealed with its two-inch barrel, the handgun was of a caliber heavy enough to have the stopping power of a larger revolver.

A pair of mongrels barked at her as she

left the buildings of Wolf Ridge behind. The eastern sky along the flat horizon became a glare as the morning sun came up. Molly pulled the brim of her Stetson down to shield her eyes. She was dressed for riding, with high-heeled boots, a divided denim skirt, and a cotton print blouse.

This vast land was cut by ravines radiating from a series of rock-crested buttes far to the south. She looked back there as the horse plodded along on a northward course. The flat-topped buttes, she'd heard, had once been inhabited by wolves, giving the town its name. The ravines were dry, as was most of this land, and the scarcity of water made for sparse grazing. For that reason the ranches of eastern Montana were huge, allowing cattle to range far in search of food.

When she came to a fork in the road, Molly remembered the Bar S Bar freight wagons she had seen in town yesterday. Deep ruts left by the wheels of loaded wagons curved off to a ranch road, and impressed into the damp earth were tracks left by the big hooves of draft horses. Molly followed them.

The ranch road was softened by melted snow that ran in rivulets in the wheel ruts, but the soil was not churned to soupy mud as the main street of Wolf Ridge had been. Here the earth was dark and wet, and the horse's hooves tossed up clods as he walked.

Molly unbuttoned her jacket to the warming sun. The air carried a fragrance of spring, and the sky overhead was pure blue. Molly saw a small black cloud of sparrows fly past, landing in a thicket on the bank of a nearby ravine. Chattering, the birds darted from branch to branch in a frantic search for insects.

Molly stopped early for her noon meal. A range of hills had come into view, and between here and there the terrain dropped off into a hidden valley. Molly saw a haze of smoke above it. After eating a roast-beef sandwich and dried fruit, she rode on. An hour and a half later she saw ranch buildings in the shallow valley, where a mess-hall stovepipe trailed a column of smoke.

Descending the slope of the valley, Molly saw an orderly arrangement of barns and sheds, pole corrals, a long bunkhouse near the mess hall, and several stockponds. Near these ponds in separately fenced pastures were bulls and purebred horses. Molly saw half a dozen Percherons and several Arabians.

Two hundred yards away in a cottonwood grove was the ranch house, an imposing rectangular structure built of white stone. The house was surrounded by a whitewashed picket fence, and as Molly rode toward the house she saw that the fence protected a garden and several flower beds where the soil was freshly turned.

Molly rode to the hitching post by the gate, dismounted, and tied the reins. She entered the yard and went to the door, seeing a calico cat reclining in a sunny window. Molly twisted the brass handle in the middle of the door and heard the doorbell ring musically inside. Moments later the door was opened by a uniformed maid.

"Ma'am?" she said, obviously surprised by the presence of a visitor.

"I've come to talk to Mr. Streeter," Molly said. "Is he here?"

"No, ma'am," the maid replied. "He's out riding with the hands —"

"Who is it, Jane?"

The woman's voice from within bore an unmistakable tone of authority. She moved into the entryway behind the maid, who turned and ducked her head in deference to the lady of the house.

"This lady, ma'am," Jane said with a Scottish brogue. "She's here to see Mr. Streeter."

The woman came forward. Molly saw that she was a handsome woman in her late thirties, with gleaming auburn hair pinned up in stylish fashion. Her face was triangular with sharp cheekbones under dark eyes and a small, heart-shaped mouth. She gazed at Molly, clearly measuring her in a competitive way. As the maid backed away, she spoke.

"I am Mrs. Streeter. May I inquire what your business is with my husband?"

Molly did not miss the note of challenge in her voice. She smiled and replied, "I was told in town that the Bar S Bar hired more men every spring than any ranch in eastern Montana, so I thought this would be a good place to start."

"Start what?" Mrs. Streeter asked.

Molly reached into her handbag and pulled out the photographic portrait. She held it out for Mrs. Streeter to see. "I'm searching for my husband."

"Oh, my," Mrs. Streeter said, looking at the portrait, then at Molly.

"He may be working as a cowhand," Molly said, "and I thought this would be a good place to start looking for him."

"I'm afraid I can't be of help," Mrs. Streeter said. "My husband does all the hiring, of course, and some of the men in line camps I never see." She looked at the photograph again and shook her head. "I assure you, I haven't seen this man. But that doesn't mean he hasn't ridden through here."

"I understand," Molly said. She looked out toward the open range past the ranch buildings. "Can you tell me where I might find Mr. Streeter or your ranch foreman?"

"No, I can't," she said slowly. "Both my husband and Buster Welch are out gathering horses for spring roundup. They could be anywhere." She paused. "You rode here from Wolf Ridge?"

Molly turned and faced her. "Yes, I came in on the train last night." She added, "My name's Molly Owens."

Mrs. Streeter smiled. "Why don't you come in and wait? The men will ride in when they're hungry, you can be certain of that."

"I don't want to impose, Mrs. Streeter —"

"Nonsense," she said, stepping back. "Come in, and we'll have a cup of tea. And call me Helene."

The ranch house was luxuriously furnished, with a touch of practicality. The entryway was not carpeted, and neither was the stairway, where Molly saw a carved newel post at the base of the bannister. She followed Helene Streeter into the front parlor, where the upholstered furniture was blue in color, matching the heavy curtains pulled back from the windows. A cutglass chandelier hung from the high ceiling.

Helene showed Molly to a sofa near the hearth of the marble fireplace and then stepped into the arched doorway on the other side of the room and asked her maid to serve tea. The water must have been on the stove. Moments later Jane came in with a teapot and cups — bone china, Molly noticed — and a plate of small sugar cookies.

"Your home is beautiful," Molly said, looking around the parlor. An oil portrait of a young man and woman hung on the far wall, and as Molly gazed at it she realized she was seeing Helene Streeter fifteen or twenty years ago. Standing behind her with a hand on her shoulder was a thick-necked man with close-cropped hair and an intense expression in his eyes.

Helene acknowledged Molly's compliment with a critical look around the room, as though searching for dust or cobwebs. "We came to Montana eighteen years ago and built this house when my husband intended to raise horses out here — and a family." She paused. "As it turned out, we only have a big cattle ranch."

Molly watched as she raised the teacup to her small mouth. Her hand quivered.

"It gets lonely out here at times," Helene went on. "That's why I'm glad to have your company, even though I know you didn't come here to make conversation. I try to get into town every so often and stay a night or two. Last week the Decency League staged a drama, and the rehearsals gave me the excuse I needed to spend time with friends."

"You're modest," Molly said. "You were the star of the production."

Helene raised her eyebrows, smiling.

"I saw the playbill at the community hall," Molly explained.

"When I was a little girl," Helene said, "I wanted to be in the theater. Oh, how much I wanted to dress up and play-act." She glanced around the parlor. "But I grew up."

In the afternoon the Bar S Bar cowhands returned to the home ranch. At the sound of hoofbeats, Helene excused herself and went to the kitchen.

Molly went to a side window and saw the men ride in. They were led by a stocky man in range clothes who rode a graceful, cream-colored Arabian horse.

The cowhands reined up at a corral near the largest barn. Leading their mounts through the gate, they stripped them and carried saddles and gear into the barn. From there they trooped to a pump by the bunkhouse and washed up for supper. The stocky man came directly to the house.

After the back door opened and closed, Molly heard the subdued voices of husband and wife. Moments later Helene returned to the parlor. A pace behind her, bareheaded now, was the stocky, bull-necked man Molly recognized from the portrait on the wall.

"Molly, this is my husband —"

Before he could be introduced, Sam Streeter charged past his wife and came to Molly with short, powerful strides.

"Howdy," he said brusquely. "Let me see this picture you're carrying."

Helene looked past him and said rather lamely, "I explained to Sam why you're here, Molly."

Molly took the photograph out of her handbag and put it in Sam Streeter's outstretched hand. He studied it, then shook his head.

"Never seen him before," he said, thrusting the photograph back at her. "Your husband run off, did he?"

"Sam," Helene said softly. She cast an apologetic smile at Molly.

"He came out this way looking for work," Molly said. "I haven't heard from him in months —"

"Your husband ever work as a cowhand?" Streeter interrupted.

Molly nodded. "He could do most anything when it came to handling horses and cattle."

"Sounds like a man I could use," Streeter said. "But he hasn't been on the place."

"Perhaps Buster should look at the photograph," Helene suggested.

Sam Streeter said, "He oughta be back from town by now. I give him a day off to go in with the wagons, and he takes two." He shrugged. "You want to wait?"

"Of course, she will," Helene said. "She's having supper with us, Sam."

"No," Molly said, "I really don't want to impose."

"I insist," Helene said. "You can't ride all the way back to town tonight. You might just as well stay over. When our ranch foreman gets back, we'll show the picture to him. He knows a lot of cowhands in Montana. If he hasn't seen your husband, then we'll pass it through the bunkhouse. Perhaps one of the hands will recognize him."

"I appreciate your help," Molly said.

"Not at all," she said. "I don't get many visitors out here, and I'm glad to have your company."

"Well, ladies," Sam Streeter announced, "if you've got this thing all figured out, I'll go take a bath, and then we'll eat."

Three-quarters of an hour later Molly was in the kitchen helping Helene and Jane dish up the meal when a horseman came riding in at a gallop.

"That'll be Buster," Helene said without looking out the window. "He always rides hard."

A moment later Molly heard booted feet thump down the front staircase. The front door opened, and Streeter shouted, "Buster! Come in here a minute!"

Molly left the kitchen and picked up her handbag in the front parlor. Taking out the photograph, she went to the entryway, where Streeter stood on the porch.

Molly looked out the open door past the square shoulders of the ranchman. She saw the rider turn his horse and ride to the picket fence. Seeing his wide-brimmed hat with the round crown, Molly immediately recognized him. The Bar S Bar foreman was the man she had left in the muddy main street of Wolf Ridge the day before.

CHAPTER VI

As their eyes met, Molly realized Buster Welch was just as surprised to see her. He had dismounted and come up the walk when he looked past Streeter. He stopped in midstride, his eyes widened.

"Buster, this lady's hunting her husband," Sam Streeter said. "Here's his picture. Ever seen him? He's worked as a cowhand."

Buster pulled his gaze away from Molly and looked at the photograph she held. "No," he said slowly, "I don't reckon I have." He looked up at his boss.

"Take this picture and pass it around the bunkhouse," Streeter said. "See if any of the boys might have ridden with him."

Buster nodded. He reached out and took the photographic portrait from Molly's hand, stealing a glance at her.

"Bring it back after you've had your supper," Sam Streeter said. "I'll see you in my office. We need to have us a talk."

Streeter backed into the entryway and closed the door. He led Molly into the dining room off the front parlor, where Jane had just set a porcelain tureen of soup on the table. He seated Molly across from Helene, then pulled out the armchair at the head of the table and sat down. He bowed his head.

"Almighty God, bless this food, this day, and let us continue your holy work, amen." He looked up at Helene. "Buster says he hasn't seen him."

She nodded and cast a sympathetic look at Molly.

"The truth is," Molly said, "I don't know what side of the law my husband is on. He may not want to be found."

Sam Streeter had motioned for Jane to serve the soup, and now as his gaze swung to Molly, his arm was held in midair.

"Young lady," he said slowly lowering his arm, "I don't know what you may have heard about the Bar S Bar Ranch, but I assure you that I do not hire criminals to work here."

"I didn't mean to suggest that," Molly said. "I was thinking that with all the far-flung line camps in the big ranches of eastern Montana, a man who wanted to hide could easily do it."

Streeter acknowledged the point with a terse nod of his head, then signaled Jane to serve the soup. It was clam chowder made from clams packed in ice that had been shipped in by rail. The rest of the meal was a feast of prime ribs, vegetables, buttery rolls with currant jam, and a dessert of hot apple pie and freshly churned ice cream.

After the meal Streeter poured coffee. He asked Molly, "If you don't get a lead on your husband, where will you go from here?"

"He may not be working on a cattle ranch," Molly said. "He may have taken up a section of land on the railroad right-of-way. He was looking for a fresh start, and he'd heard about the land giveaway —"

"Fresh start," Streeter growled. "Those farmers are being lured here by Preston Brooks. Ever heard of him? Most folks have, I reckon. He owns the North American & Pacific Railroad, and he thinks he owns Montana. He's bringing farmers in here under false pretenses. He tells them they'll make a go of it, get a fresh start, like you say.

"But the truth of the matter is that Brooks is bringing folks into this country to generate business for his railroad. Those farm families will be here for a few seasons, long enough to figure out this isn't farm country, and then they'll leave. And they'll leave behind hundreds of acres of range land ruined by the plow. In the meantime Brooks will have made money off them and everybody else who got suckered into coming out here."

Streeter's face had reddened while he spoke, and now he pushed his chair back and stood. Muttering that he had to look after a Percheron foal in the barn, he snatched his hat off a peg in the wall and strode out of the dining room. A moment later the back door slammed shut.

In his wake was a heavy silence, at last broken as Helene ventured a smile at Molly and suggested they take their coffee into the parlor.

Her subdued mood changed after her husband's departure, Molly noticed. Now she once again became the lady of the house and took on an air of authority. She impatiently rang a small silver bell that summoned the maid. When Jane appeared, her hands wet with dishwater, Helene ordered her to make up the bed in an upstairs bedroom and then carry water up there and fill the basin.

Molly saw a harried look on the maid's face as she ducked her head and retreated to the kitchen. "Let me help," Molly said. "I can make up that bed —"

"Nonsense," Helene said, flashing a smile at her. "Let Jane do the work I pay her to do."

The evening passed with Helene relating to Molly the history of their ranch, how she and Sam had come here as a young couple and chosen this spot to build their home. The times had been hard, but good, Helene said as she told of hunting deer and elk herself when Sam was too busy with the everyday problems of managing the big ranch.

"I can hardly see myself doing that sort of thing anymore," Helene said, sighing. "Such things are always better to look back on."

Evening light had thinned to darkness when the back door opened. Sam Streeter came in, followed by Buster Welch. Buster went on to his boss's office, a room off the main hall that Molly had spotted earlier, and Sam came into the parlor carrying the photograph.

"Nobody's seen him," he said.

Molly thanked him for his help, and received a cool look in reply. The ranchman turned away and went to his office. Molly heard the door close.

A quarter of an hour later that door opened. Buster Welch hurried out of the house. Presently Streeter came out and stopped in the arched doorway of the front parlor.

"Well," he said, "early to bed, early to rise." With a hard look at Helene, he walked away.

Hearing the man's heavy footsteps on the stairs, Molly set her coffee cup down and said, "I'm ready for bed, too."

Helene smiled. "I'll take you to your room, and make certain Jane has done everything properly." She paused and added, "I really must apologize for Sam —"

"I'm the one who should apologize," Molly said. "I believe I offended him."

"The Bar S Bar Ranch borders the North American & Pacific right-of-way," Helene explained. "Sam sees red at the mention of Preston Brooks."

Molly saw an enigmatic look come into Helene Streeter's eyes as she spoke, one that might have been an expression of triumph.

The moment passed when she stood and took Molly upstairs to a spare bedroom. After wishing Helene good night, Molly closed the door. The room, wall-papered in a vine and flower pattern, was simply furnished with oak furniture and a four-poster bed with a canopy.

Molly undressed, blew out the lamp, and climbed into the bed. She stared up at the darkened canopy, thinking about what she had seen today. Sam and Helene Streeter lived a sumptuous life here, enjoying luxuries Molly would not have guessed were available to them.

Yet happiness cannot be bought, as the saying went, and the tension between man and wife was unmistakable. On the surface all was perfect, but this evening Molly had glimpsed beneath that smooth surface and seen turmoil.

She fell asleep after reminding herself that she was not here to investigate domestic troubles but to find out if the Bar S Bar Ranch was harboring outlaws. Sam Streeter impressed her as a man of action. Now she wondered if he had taken violent actions against the North American & Pacific Railroad.

After breakfast at daybreak Molly asked the ranchman for permission to ride out to his line camps and show the photograph to the other Bar S Bar cowhands. Streeter shook his head in reply.

"It isn't safe for a woman to ride the range alone," he said, "and I can't spare a man to go with you."

"I could ride with her, Sam," Helene said.

Streeter cast a glance in her direction, then shook his head again. "It isn't safe for two women, either. Besides, those cowhands are out working during the day, so all you'd find are empty line shacks." He picked up his coffee cup and drained it.

"No, Miss Owens," he went on, "I believe you'll do best in your search if you ride back to Wolf Ridge." He stood, adding, "And stay there."

Molly watched as he turned his back to her, took his hat off the peg in the wall, and left the room. Helene lowered her head until the back door closed.

She smiled weakly. "Seems like I'm always apologizing for him."

"No need," Molly said. "I can understand a rancher not wanting strangers riding through his property — particularly women strangers."

"Where will you go from here?" she asked.

"Back to Wolf Ridge," Molly said, "for the time being. I'll ask around town, and then I'll probably ride out to some other ranches."

"I will be coming to town in a few days," Helene said. "May I look you up?"

"Of course," Molly said. "I'm staying at The Montanan."

"Preston Brooks' hotel," Helene said musingly. After a pause, she added, "I

63

want to help you, Molly. I don't know how I can help you yet, but maybe we can think of a way."

Helene sent Jane running to the barn with word to have Molly's horse saddled and brought to the front gate. After Molly thanked her for her hospitality, she walked out to the picket fence. Her horse was led from the barn by Buster Welch.

"So you're hunting your husband," he said when he reached her at the gate. He held the horse's reins in a gloved hand while regarding her. "What if you don't find him?"

Molly did not reply, but moved a step closer and reached out for the reins.

Buster pulled back and held them out of her reach. "I figured you'd say something about me to Streeter," he said. "But you didn't, did you?"

"Give me the reins, Buster," Molly said.

He grinned cockily. "You look like you need a good man."

Molly made a pretext of looking around. "I don't see any."

"Lady," he growled, "you've got a smart mouth on you."

Meeting his angry stare, Molly held out her hand for the horse's reins. Buster abruptly dropped them and stepped away.

Molly retrieved the reins and moved to the left side of the horse. She thrust her boot in the stirrup and swung up into the saddle.

"One of these days," Buster said, "we'll meet again." He squinted against the morning sun. "You just watch."

"I always watch out for coyotes and wolves, Buster," Molly said. Touching her heels to the horse, she rode away.

CHAPTER VII

In the following days Molly showed the photographic portrait in every saloon and gambling house in Wolf Ridge, and she rode out to the headquarters of half a dozen ranches in the area. At midnight exactly one week after her arrival she left The Montanan by a back staircase that led to an alley.

Molly followed the alley toward the depot, hearing night sounds from the saloon district on the next street. Main Street was empty and silent. By starlight she saw the water tower ahead. Drawing closer, she heard water dripping into puddles beneath it.

On a siding across the way she saw the dull gleam and shadowy shape of a locomotive. Steam was up, and the big engine hissed like some strange, menacing animal of the night. A tender and two private cars with curtains drawn were behind it. Cinders crunching underfoot, Molly stepped over the tracks of the main line and headed for the cars.

"Right on time."

Preston Brooks spoke as he stepped out of the deep shadows between the two cars.

Taking Molly by the arm, he led her up the back steps of the rear car and opened the door. Lamplight streamed out.

Molly stepped into the band of light and entered the car. Her feet sank into thick carpet. Brooks came in behind her and pulled the door shut.

"Drink?" he asked. "I have some good brandy." He motioned toward a glassed case stocked with tall bottles.

Molly shook her head as she glanced around the luxuriously furnished car. Memories of awakening in this paneled railroad coach rushed into her mind.

"Business before pleasure," he said with a quick grin. He gestured to a pair of chairs upholstered in soft, chocolate-colored leather. "Let me hear your report."

Molly sat down and gave him a brief summary of her investigation during the past week. She listed all the ranches she had visited and named the cattlemen and ranch foremen she had spoken to; then she gave him a rundown of the saloons and gambling houses in Wolf Ridge where she had interviewed dozens of men, several of whom she had recognized from wanted posters.

"What's your conclusion?" he asked.

"Simply this, Mr. Brooks —"

"Pres," he reminded her.

"Pres," she said, "you're a hated man in this part of Montana."

Brooks stared at her, then threw his head back and laughed.

"You may not be aware of the intensity of feeling against you," Molly said. "Every rancher and cowhand I talked to is convinced you're bringing ruin to the state."

"I'm perfectly aware of their sentiment," he said, still smiling. "I didn't have to hire an investigator to learn that." He paused and went on, "Perhaps you've also learned that many influential people in Wolf Ridge support me and what I'm trying to do — which is to bring prosperity to a bleak land. The same holds true in other towns along my rail line."

Molly did not openly disagree, but she believed he overestimated the number of "influential people" who supported his cause. This was cattle country from horizon to horizon, and the ranchers had much more power than a few storekeepers and farmers.

"The question is," Brooks continued, "which of these reactionary cattlemen are harboring train robbers?"

"I can't prove that any of them are," Molly said. "Not yet. But I do know that ranchers who are otherwise law-abiding would have few qualms about protecting outlaws."

Brooks nodded.

"You were right about Sam Streeter," Molly said. "He's a strong-willed man, and the other cattlemen look to him for leadership. If I were to continue my investigation, I'd focus on the Bar S Bar." She added, "A joke going around town is that any man who's out of work will find a job on the Bar S Bar if he can prove he's robbed an NA&P train."

Brooks pursed his lips. "I want you to go ahead with the investigation. What's your next move?"

"I've struck up an acquaintance with Streeter's wife," Molly said. "She offered to direct me to Bar S Bar line camps."

"Behind Sam Streeter's back?" he asked.

Molly nodded.

Brooks grinned. "I'm impressed with your work, Molly. You've pounded a lot of shoe and saddle leather in the last week. Horace Fenton was right when he told me you were the best operative for this job. You've come up with a ruse that allows you to go anywhere and ask questions without stirring folks up."

Brooks stood and looked at her with admiration. "Now, about that brandy. Will you join me and have a snifter?"

"Yes," Molly said with a smile, "I'd like that."

He went to the liquor cabinet and opened one of the glassed doors. Goblets and snifters stood in a rack there. He took two out, and lifted a squat, long-necked bottle off a shelf.

"By the way," he said, puffing the cork out of the brandy bottle, "I'm opening a homestead locator office here."

Brooks brought a snifter to Molly and sat down. "Now that spring is here, I'll start bringing settlers in. A few settled on my right-of-way last year, but more will come this time. My advertisements in the U.S. and Europe are bringing results. People are lining up for their free train tickets to come out here."

He swirled the dark liquid in the glass, watching it absently while he spoke. "I'm bringing my right-hand man out here to run things. Name's Asa Lemmon. I'll tell him you're here, and any messages can be sent to me through him."

Molly drank from her snifter, feeling the liquor course warmly down her throat. "Is that wise?"

"You can trust Asa," Brooks said. "He's

tight-lipped, and tough as a spike. He'll be a valuable ally for you."

"I prefer to work alone, Pres," Molly said.

He said with a quick grin, "Always?"

"I was talking about business, Pres," she said, "not pleasure."

He laughed heartily.

Molly downed the brandy and set the snifter on the polished walnut top of an elaborately carved side table. She stood. Brooks got to his feet. He moved close to her, not saying anything, but Molly saw a certain look in his eyes.

"When do you want my next report?" Molly asked.

"As soon as Asa gets here," he said. "He'll relay all your reports to me from now on."

A husky tone had deepened his voice. Molly looked into his eyes. They shone with the light of the lamps. He reached out and took her hand. Molly knew he was on the edge of saying something to her, words of intimacy. But then he seemed to catch himself.

"Be careful, Molly," he whispered. "This is a dangerous business you're in."

She nodded, not taking her eyes from his. She did not pull back when he leaned down and kissed her. As their lips touched, he embraced her.

Molly wrapped her arms around his shoulders, returning his kiss. The sensation of his mustache was sensuous to her and surprisingly erotic. Her arousal built within her like an engine building a head of steam, and she held him tightly, her breasts pressing against him. She felt his warmth and strength as their mouths opened and his tongue probed hers. His breath came hotly and deeply, and Molly knew his passion was mounting. But then he broke off the kiss.

Molly let go and stepped back. "Something's wrong."

Pres drew a long breath, looking at her with an expression tinged with sorrow.

"You have a wife waiting for you in Chicago," she suggested.

He smiled weakly. "No, it's a bit more complicated than that."

"Oh," Molly said.

"Damn," he said in a low voice, "but you're a beautiful woman. You make me laugh, you make me feel so damned alive. I have this awful feeling that you're the woman I've been waiting for all these years. But now I can't . . . ." His voice trailed off.

"I'd better leave," Molly said. She went to the door.

"Molly," he said helplessly.

She turned to face him. For once he seemed without words to explain a predicament. "I'll wait until I hear from you, then?"

"Yes," he said. "I'll . . . I'll be in touch."

Molly turned away and pulled the coach door open. She stepped outside. When the door closed, she was alone, surrounded by darkness.

She left the rail yard and walked between the dripping water tower and depot as she gingerly made her way back to the alley. In the week since she had arrived in Wolf Ridge the sunny and warm days had dried the muddy streets, leaving them wrinkled with deep ruts.

By starlight Molly picked her way through the ruts and entered the back alley between Main Street and the saloon district. She heard piano music from a dance hall, and the off-key singing of a drunken woman. The woman was silenced by a chorus of laughter.

A sudden whisper of movement alerted Molly, but she did not have time to draw her revolver when she was hit from behind. Knocked to the ground, a big, foul-

73

smelling man came down on top of her, hard.

Cupping a callused hand over her mouth, he spoke into her ear. "Don't holler out, and I won't hurt you."

His breath reeked of whiskey. Molly bit down on his hand. He howled.

"Damn you!" He raised up and slugged her, his fist slamming into the side of her head.

Molly's ears rang with the blow. A wave of sleepy dizziness swept over her, and as his great weight rested on top of her, she felt a sickening fear that she would not be able to stop him.

"I'll hurt you bad if you do that again," he said in a rough whisper. Moving off, he turned her over. He held her by pushing one hand down on her throat. With his other hand he pulled her dress up past her thighs.

"Smooth legs," he muttered.

Molly could not draw a breath as the man's hand probed between her legs. Then he grasped her underclothes and yanked, tearing them away.

CHAPTER VIII

The man forced her legs apart with his knees. Molly wanted to resist, but her consciousness was slipping away. She heard roaring in her ears, and a strangely peaceful blackness was closing in. Stars in the sky blurred.

Suddenly the hand pressing down on her throat was gone. Molly gasped. Her lungs filled with cool air. Blinking against tears, she saw the bulky figure in the starlight. She realized the man was on his knees now, unbuttoning his trousers.

Molly slid a hand under her jacket. She gripped the handle of her revolver. Pulling it out of the shoulder holster, she fought her instinct to shoot this beast. A gunshot would bring a night deputy running, and right now she did not want to have to explain what she was doing here this time of night.

"You're gonna like this," he said, lowering himself down on her. "Ain't no need to fight it."

Molly moved her hand down the length of the revolver, grasping the barrel. The man was intent on gaining position, and did not see her hand raise up high over his head.

Using the gun like a hammer, she timed the blow to meet her attacker's head as he leaned forward and came down on top of her. The gun butt struck him with a dull *thunk*. He groaned.

For a moment the man did not move. Then like a confused bull he shook his head. Molly hit him again, hammering his head as hard as she could, and this time he slumped down, falling limply on her.

Molly pushed and shifted enough of his weight to one side that she was able to get out from under him. She raised to her knees, breathing in great gulps of air. In the distance music came from a brass band in a dance hall on the next street.

Her attacker lay still with his trousers around his knees. His bare buttocks were two pale spheres in the starlight. He breathed deeply, as though asleep.

Recovered, Molly quickly searched through the man's pockets. He carried nothing but a pocket knife, some wadded bills, and a few coins. Clearly, he was a drifter and had probably ridden the rods of freight car to get here.

Back in her room on the second floor of The Montanan, Molly undressed and washed. Violated but not raped, she felt unclean. Her torn underclothes lay in a heap where she had dropped them on the floor, and now she picked them up and angrily threw them into a trash basket in a corner of the room.

She had defeated her attacker, but still she was angry she had not been able to give him the least of what he deserved — an arrest and a jail term. Knowing that she could not do anything to compromise her investigation was little consolation. She had always told herself that her profession came first, that she must carry out the job she had agreed to do, and now she was forced to live with that commitment.

In the morning Molly wore a high-necked dress when she left her room and descended the stairs to the hotel dining room. The dress, brown with a collar edged by fine lace, covered the dark bruise at her throat.

She had ordered scrambled eggs, bacon, and a hot biscuit with honey for breakfast when a familiar voice spoke her name. She looked up to see Helene Streeter approaching.

"Good morning," the ranch woman said. "I warned you that I'd look you up. May I join you?"

"Of course," Molly said. "Sit down.

Have you had breakfast?"

Helene pulled out a chair and sat in it. She wore an elegant dress of silk and a hat topped with red and yellow silk flowers, and she carried a parasol.

"The truth is," she said confidentially, "I'm not supposed to set foot in this place. It's owned by you know who." She smiled at this disobedience of her husband's law.

Molly returned the smile. "I'll keep the secret, Helene."

"I came in here because I am ravenously hungry," she said, "and this is the best restaurant in town." She added, "And I hoped to run into you."

Molly raised her coffee cup in a toast. "Good fortune." She signaled the waitress.

After ordering her breakfast, Helene said, "Speaking of good fortune, have you had any in your search?"

"No, I haven't," Molly said. She recounted her activities over the past week.

"You've been busy," Helene said. "You certainly have a lot of nerve to go into all the saloons in town."

Molly smiled. "I quit worrying about my reputation long ago."

"Perhaps I should, too," Helene mused. She asked, "What are your plans now?"

"I'll stay until I'm satisfied he isn't

here," Molly said. "He could be working on any of the ranches around here. If he's grown a beard, or even a mustache, people might not recognize his picture."

Helene said, "If you want to check the Bar S Bar line camps, my offer to help is still good."

"I don't want to be the cause of any trouble —"

"Oh, don't worry yourself," Helene said. "Sam talks tough, but I can handle him." She added, "In fact, if we leave right after breakfast, I can drive you to the south line camp today."

"If you go with me," Molly said, "your husband will hear of it from the cowhands."

Helene shrugged. "With Sam, I've found it easier to get forgiveness than permission."

After breakfast they ordered box lunches, and at midmorning Molly sat beside Helene on the tufted leather seat of her top buggy. The buggy was black with a brass night light mounted on the cowl, and the spokes of the high wheels were painted red. The vehicle was pulled by a beautiful Arabian gelding.

From the livery barn Helene crossed the main street of town, passing between a bank and a church with a tall steeple. The street she followed paralleled the railroad tracks. On the other side was a granary and a sprawling lumber yard.

At the edge of Wolf Ridge the street became a narrow road that ran east beside the tracks. The tops of the steel rails, polished by two freight trains a day and three passenger trains a week, gleamed in the morning sunlight.

The day was going to be warm and clear, Molly saw as she looked around. The land here was rolling, marked by low ridges where creeks and dry washes cut through the rocky soil. In the distance she saw a herd of antelope. The lead buck watched them approach, then turned his white rump and bounded away. The others followed, disappearing over a grassy rise.

The road angled in that direction. A quarter of an hour later the buggy topped the rise, and Molly saw a homesteader's cabin and plowed field in the small valley below. A pair of mules grazed nearby.

"All of this land is the NA&P right-of-way," Helene said with a sweep of her outstretched arm. The gesture took in the valley to the north and the flat expanse of land to the south where railroad tracks made a straight line to the east.

"Where's your land from here?" Molly asked.

Helene pointed down to the valley. "Bar S Bar range begins at the far edge of that plowed field." She gestured up the length of the valley. "Other homesteads are up there, too. Last year these farmers got a good crop of wheat — fifty bushels to the acre, we heard."

As she drove along the top of the rise, she went on, "Sam isn't worried about a few homesteaders like the ones who have taken over this little piece of ground. He's worried that if a few make it, others will come. Preston Brooks wants to bring thousands of farmers to this country, and you know how Sam feels about that." She cast a glance at Molly.

In the next two hours they passed more than a dozen homesteads in the valley. The cabins had been supplied by Brooks and all looked alike — twenty-four by twenty-four feet, built of green lumber that was already starting to warp. Several had tarpaper tacked to the walls in an attempt to ward off the frigid winds of winter that blew down from Canada.

As the homesteaded land fell behind, the road dwindled to little more than a pair of wheel ruts through weeds and tufts of grass. Helene explained that this was a Bar S Bar road, one that was used to resupply the line camp several times a year.

After stopping to eat their box lunch, they drove on, following the dim tracks into low hills that lay north of the homesteaded valley and the railroad tracks. The hills concealed Bar S Bar cattle.

The range-wise cattle had survived the winter in the protected gullies and ravines in these hills and were not inclined to be herded out and moved northward into summer pastures. The cowhands who worked out of the line camp in this sector of the ranch methodically combed each hidden gully and ravine, often driving out only a few head at a time. Some stout bulls stood their ground and pawed the earth, and it took a skilled man on a nimble horse to move these stubborn animals.

Molly knew that Sam Streeter had been right when he told her there was no point in visiting a line camp during daylight hours. All the cowhands would be out on the range.

But in her experience as a Fenton operative, Molly had met few outlaws who were willing to clean out water holes, repair fences, or doctor cattle or who even possessed a cowhand's skills. If a gang of train robbers was being harbored on this ranch, she expected to find them idly passing the time in a line camp.

Early in the afternoon Helene pointed ahead. Molly saw a haze of smoke in the sky. A quarter of an hour later the buggy topped a hill overlooking a small coulee. In the bottom of the coulee she saw a pair of cabins, some sheds, and a pole corral holding half a dozen horses. Smoke drifted out of the black stovepipe in the roof of the nearest cabin.

Helene drove the buggy downslope toward the line camp, and one of the horses in the corral whinnied. The door of the near cabin immediately swung open. A man stepped out, and two others shouldered into the doorway behind him.

The man stood with his hands on his hips, watching. He was armed with a revolver in a cutaway holster strapped to his leg. As the buggy drew closer, the man grinned. He pushed his Stetson up on his forehead and came out to meet the buggy.

"Howdy, ladies. If you were sent out here to entertain lonely men, you came to the right place."

Molly tensed, staring at the grinning, bug-eyed man. There was no mistaking his squeaky voice, and now she recognized his face. He was the outlaw who had aimed and fired his rifle at her, one of the pair who had ambushed her and killed Oliver Newman.

CHAPTER IX

"I beg your pardon," Helene said, climbing out of the buggy.

Molly followed, reaching into her handbag to grasp the handle of her Colt .38.

"My husband is Sam Streeter," Helene said as she approached the man. "Do you men work for the Bar S Bar?"

The bug-eyed man's grin faded quickly. "Well, uh, no ma'am. We're, uh, riding the grub line. Mr. Streeter, he said we could stay over a few days." He added, "Ask him, if you like."

"That won't be necessary," Helene said crisply. "This lady is looking for a certain man. It's very important that she find him. He may be riding the grub line, too, and she'd like to know if you've seen him."

"What's he look like?" he asked, his gaze moving to Molly.

Molly let go of the gun. She found the photographic portrait in her handbag and handed it to him. Their eyes met. She saw no sign of recognition. The man's expression did not change when he studied the picture, and when he looked at Molly again he shook his head.

"No, I ain't never seen him," he said.

"Maybe your friends have," Helene said.

He nodded and turned around. Molly watched as he walked back to the cabin door, and she put her hand on the gun in her handbag.

"Saddle tramps," Helene said under her breath. "I don't know why Sam gives them the time of day, much less room and board."

While the photograph was being passed between the men in the cabin doorway, Helene went on, "Of course, Sam says if we don't feed them, they'll steal our stock. Horses, too. So maybe this is the cheapest way to get rid of tramps."

A third man in the cabin examined the picture, and then the bug-eyed outlaw brought it back to Molly. "We ain't seen him, ma'am, none of us."

Molly took it from his hand. The killer had not even recognized his victim. Before her eyes could reveal her thoughts, Molly turned away. She strode back to the buggy. Helene followed, climbing in after her.

Driving away from the line camp, Helene said, "I do believe you took a strong dislike to that man, Molly."

Molly tried to pass it off with a casual shrug and a weak smile. But her heart pounded in her chest.

"I didn't like the way he leered at us, either," Helene said. She slapped the reins down on the sorrel, urging the horse up the slope.

They reached Wolf Ridge at nightfall. A freight train was pulling onto the siding by the big lumber yard, and as Helene drove past the cars Molly caught the fresh scent of cut wood. Helene turned on the main street and stopped in front of The Montanan.

"Thanks for all your help today," Molly said to her.

"I'm just sorry you didn't find the answer you were looking for," she said.

Molly jerked her head toward the plate-glass window of the hotel restaurant. "Will you join me for dinner? The least I can do is —"

"I'd love to, but I can't," Helene said. "I'm staying in town with friends, and they're expecting me."

Late that night Molly lay in bed, fists and jaw clenched. This afternoon she had needed all of her self-control to keep from pulling her gun on that grinning murderer.

Seeing him at the line camp brought back the memory of Oliver Newman's death, and now as she went to sleep she relived those terrifying moments in the frozen, white land. The silence had been shattered by gunfire, and Oliver Newman, his mouth open as he was ready to say something, was shot out of the saddle. An instant later Molly smashed into the snowbank, unable to breathe, pain seeping through her chest. The dream was real.

The hand slowly closing over her mouth was no dream, and Molly came out of a deep sleep, staring into darkness.

"Don't scream."

The hand pulled away. Molly raised up on her elbows. "Pres?"

"None other," Preston Brooks said, sitting on the edge of the bed.

Molly pushed a lock of hair out of her face, now seeing his shadowy form. "How did you —"

"It's my hotel, remember?" he said. "I used my key to let myself in through the back door. Sorry if I scared you, but I don't want anyone to know I'm in town."

"Pres," Molly said, coming fully awake now, "outlaws are using the south line camp on the Bar S Bar."

In a tense voice he asked, "You're certain?"

"Yes," Molly said. She described the buggy ride she had taken with Helene

Streeter and the bug-eyed outlaw she recognized at the line camp. "They claimed to be cowhands riding the grub line."

Brooks said in a tense voice, "I'll get the bastards. And I'll make Streeter regret this."

"First thing in the morning I'll notify Sheriff Jenkins," Molly said. "With a posse, he can —"

Brooks interrupted, "That two-bit lawman is in Sam Streeter's hip pocket. He'll ride to hell after rustlers or horse thieves, but he won't saddle his horse for train robbers. I know that for a fact."

"What are you going to do?" Molly asked.

"Get some hard riding detectives," Brooks said, "and do the sheriff's job for him."

"I'll ride with you," Molly said.

"No, you won't," Brooks said sharply. In a milder tone of voice he went on, "You can't ride after outlaws without giving away your identity. I don't want you to do that — not yet."

Molly had thought her assignment here was nearly completed. "Sounds like you have other plans for me."

"I want you to be my eyes and ears around here," he said. "Tempers are likely to flare when the homestead locator office is opened and I bring in the first trainload of prospective farmers."

"I'm an investigator, Pres," Molly said, "not a spy."

"You'll have plenty to investigate around here," he said, standing. "We'll talk about it later. Right now I have to get moving. In the next twenty-four hours I'll have to locate some detectives who aren't afraid of gunplay."

After he was gone, Molly lay back on the pillow. She was awake for a quarter of an hour or more, and heard a steam engine puff out of town. She guessed that Brooks was making a fast run to Chicago in his Silver Comet.

Preston Brooks was a man accustomed to having his way about things, but Molly had her ideas, too. She disliked being left out of the conclusion of an investigation she had started and put a lot of work into. She closed her eyes. A plan was forming in her mind as she dropped off to sleep.

Molly left Wolf Ridge after eating the noon meal in the hotel restaurant and ordering two box lunches. She crossed the street and bought a wool blanket and a two-quart canteen in Geary's Hardware &

Ranch Supply. Then she walked to the livery, where she filled the canteen at the pump and rented a saddle horse.

Molly followed the old freight road out of town. She rode alongside the tracks and then topped the rise overlooking the homesteaded valley. She continued on at a steady pace, timing her approach to the Bar S Bar line camp so that she arrived around nightfall. She left the dim road before the coulee came in sight and found a hiding place half a mile away.

In some brush at the base of the hill that concealed her from the coulee, she picketed the horse, watered him from the canteen, and left him to graze. Carrying one of the box lunches to the top of the hill. Molly bent low and peered down into the coulee.

The cabins had no windows, but she saw a glow of lamplight around the doors of both of them. By the light of stars twinkling in the black sky she saw ten or twelve horses in the corral. The cowhands were in for the night, she guessed, and so were the outlaws.

Molly sat there and ate her cold supper while watching the line camp. At first the night was silent, but after she had sat perfectly still for an hour, animals stirred.

Coyotes called to one another, howling in the distance. Howls were answered by yips, and yips were answered by high-pitched barks. She was briefly startled when an owl swooped low over her head, probably hunting field mice. In the brushy hollow behind her the saddle horse occasionally stamped a hoof.

The doors to both cabins opened from time to time, spilling out yellow light from kerosene lamps. The men came out to relieve themselves or tend the horses. In the darkness Molly could not see them clearly, but she did notice that men from one cabin never went into the other. Cowhands did not mix with outlaws, she concluded.

The day had been warm, but now the night took on a chill. Molly made her way by starlight back down the slope to the horse. She got her blanket and returned to her point of observation.

Glad now that she wore denim trousers and a warm flannel shirt, she spread the blanket on the ground. She lay down and pulled the blanket around her, looking downslope at the cabins. Presently she closed her eyes.

Lying on hard, uneven ground made for a long night. Molly slept in fits and starts, and by the first light of day she was sitting with the blanket over her shoulders, eating a roast beef sandwich and drinking from her canteen. The eastern skyline grew pink.

On the far side of the coulee nearly half a mile away she saw movement. First thinking antelope were there, she watched while chewing the last of the roast beef. Then she quickly lay down and scooted back to conceal herself. The animals she saw in the distance were horses — nine of them. Each horse was led by a man carrying a rifle.

CHAPTER X

Molly watched from the top of the rise while the nine gunmen tied their horses. On foot they advanced toward the blind side of the cabins, and spread out in a line, holding their rifles at the ready.

In Molly's field of vision she saw the door of the farthest cabin open. A cowhand wearing only boots and long underwear came out. He carried a bucket, and the gunmen did not see him until he walked sleepily to the pump beside a water trough at the corral.

The squealing and clanking of the pump drifted to Molly's ears while the cowhand worked the handle. Water gushed from the spout. Unaware of trouble, he held the bucket under the spout until a rifle barrel punched into his back.

The bucket dropped from his hand as his body stiffened, and water spilled over his boots. He raised his hands and walked at gun point behind the cabin where the other armed men waited.

Moments later Molly saw four gunmen move swiftly to the open front door of the cowhands' cabin. They dashed inside.

Presently three undressed cowhands came out, hands held high over their hatless heads, and were marched to the rear of the cabin.

With the prisoners under guard, the gunmen regrouped and made a half-circle around the near cabin. It, too, was windowless and had only the one front door, but something, some sound, must have alerted the men inside. Molly saw a puff of smoke between the logs, and heard a shot.

One of the gunmen doubled over and dropped to his knees. The others pulled back, with two grabbing the wounded man by the arms and dragging him away. They took refuge behind the other cabin, and started shooting.

More shots rang out from the cabin as the outlaws inside broke out chinking between the logs and fired at the gunmen. Molly saw smoke from gunpowder rise into the morning sky.

Then she heard shouts, and the firing stopped. A familiar voice reached her ears.

"Come out! Come out, or we'll burn you out!" The voice belonged to Preston Brooks.

He was quickly answered by a loud curse and half a dozen shots from the cabin.

Molly watched for an hour. Nothing

happened. She edged back and went down the slope to her horse. She gave him oats from a sack and water that she'd poured into her Stetson and then carried the canteen back to her observation point. For the rest of the morning she lay under the warming sun and watched the standoff. Shouts and shots were exchanged sporadically.

Molly believed she understood Brooks' plan. Keep pressure on the outlaws, and they might break and make a run for it or surrender. But time was slowly running out. Darkness would favor the trapped outlaws.

The day had worn on to midafternoon when Brooks evidently made a decision to break the stalemate. One of his gunmen came around to the front of the cowhands' cabin and darted inside. He came out carrying a kerosene lamp.

Presently Molly saw smoke drifting up behind the cabin. A smoldering gunnysack filled with weeds or hay was lofted into the air, landing at the base of the other cabin. It was immediately answered by gunshots from within. Next Molly saw the lamp tossed onto the gunnysack. It was broken by a bullet fired by one of the gunmen.

Smoke boiled up as kerosene from the lamp ran into the gunnysack. A moment later flames leaped up, licking at the weathered logs of the cabin.

The fire swept up the side of the wall. Gray and black smoke drifted into the sky. Molly watched as flames crawled around the sides of the cabin like a hungry beast devouring its prey. Then the door banged open.

The four outlaws came running out, brandishing rifles and revolvers. Molly saw immediately they had a desperate plan. The outlaws attacked, shooting as they rushed the other cabin. Behind them, their own cabin was in flames.

They were met by a volley of rifle fire, another and then another. One outlaw was flung to the ground by the impact of several bullets. Another was wounded and dropped to one knee, firing his revolver. The other two stood their ground, shooting steadily.

The scream of a dying outlaw reached Molly's ears as another went down. The one still on his feet turned and ran, leaving the man on his knees shooting a second revolver.

The fleeing outlaw ran across the flat and up the slope of the rise, straight to

Molly. She edged back, then stood and drew her Colt .38, knowing she could do nothing but confront him.

The moment the running outlaw came over the top of the rise, his eyes bugged open in amazement. He did not break stride even as Molly ordered him to halt, and in desperation he lunged down the slope, throwing himself at her.

Molly's shot missed, and she was driven back when he hit her. Together they struck the ground and rolled down the slope toward the grazing horse. Molly had lost her grip on her gun, her hat had flown off, and now her long blonde hair was unpinned.

The outlaw rolled away and came up on his knees. He stared, obviously surprised to see a woman. A second later his fist lashed out.

Molly ducked the blow and retreated, getting to her feet as he lunged for her. This time she was ready for him. She sidestepped and brought the side of her hand down on the back of his neck. He plowed into the ground, face first.

The outlaw came up on all fours, reaching back to his boot. He drew out a long, thin bladed knife, and came up to a crouching position.

"I need that horse," he said in a squeaky voice.

The sound of his voice brought Molly back to a terrifying moment when she had been sprawled out in a snow bank and saw this man raise his rifle and squint down the sights as he pulled the trigger.

Molly backed away. "You should have killed me when you had the chance," she said.

"Whatta . . . whatta you talking about?"

"You murdered a Fenton operative last month," she said, "and you shot me out of the saddle."

"By damn!" he exclaimed. "You. . . ." He did not finish, but lunged at her.

The point of the knife missed by an inch as Molly leaped away. The bug-eyed outlaw was off balance, and she kicked him. The point of her boot went deep into his midsection, doubling him over.

"Give it up," Molly said. "I'm taking you in."

He tried to straighten as he turned toward her, grimacing with rage in his eyes. He staggered toward her, waving the knife.

From over Molly's shoulder came a thundering rifle shot. The bug-eyed outlaw flopped to the ground, and slowly lay back. A bright red stain seeped across his shirt front. He lay still, bulging eyes staring up at the deep blue sky.

Molly whirled around. At the top of the rise she saw a man lowering a rifle from his shoulder.

"You fool!" Molly shouted.

He stared down at her, and a moment later a second man appeared beside him.

"Molly!"

Hands on her hips, she looked up the slope at Preston Brooks. He came plunging toward her, followed by the man carrying a Winchester rifle.

"What the hell are you doing here?" Brooks demanded.

"I thought you might need a hand," Molly replied when he reached her. "I came out to keep an eye on things."

She met his angry gaze, and glanced at the man who followed him. He was shorter, narrow shouldered, and his sideburns angled across his jaw to meet his dark mustache. He wore range clothes that might have been fresh off the shelf that day, and a city hat.

"Thanks to him," Molly said, "we don't have a man to question."

"He was going for her with a knife, Pres," the man said. "He'd have opened her up like a can of beans."

Molly shook her head. "I had him under control." The man's derisive laughter was cut short when Molly reached into the hip pocket of her trousers and brought out a two-shot derringer.

"Pres," he said, turning away from her, "all I saw was that bastard going for her with a knife."

Brooks pulled his gaze away from the dead man and raised a hand to silence the dispute. "You two might as well get acquainted. Molly, this is Asa Lemmon. Asa, meet Molly Owens, a Fenton operative who works for me." Brooks added, "She's a top-notch detective, but she doesn't take orders too well."

CHAPTER XI

Preston Brooks and his hired gunmen left the bodies where they lay and the cabin a smoldering ruin. The dazed Bar S Bar cowhands, hatless, barefooted, and clad in long johns, stood in a knot behind the other cabin, warily watching the detectives ride away.

Molly glanced back at the cowhands as she rode with the detectives. She had given the line camp a wide berth, hoping that with her hair pinned up under her Stetson and wearing denim trousers and a flannel shirt the cowhands would not realize she was a woman, one they might have seen in town.

Her rented saddle horse held the pace as Preston Brooks led the way across a grassy flat, down into a dry ravine, and up the other side toward the North American & Pacific railroad tracks. Two hours later the Silver Comet came in sight.

Molly had never seen Brooks' private train in the light of day, and now as the big locomotive loomed on the horizon Molly realized why Buck had been so excited when she mentioned she had ridden in a private car owned by the tycoon.

The steam engine, a ten-wheeler with a diamond-shaped smokestack was black with nickel-plated fittings, wheels, and drivers. It pulled a tender, four private coaches, and a stock car ahead of the bright red caboose.

Steam was up, and when they reached the waiting train and dismounted, Molly saw this train was manned by a uniformed conductor, an engineer and a fireman, a chef and two waiters who leaned out of the dining car, and a man who loaded the horses in the stock car.

The gunmen strode to the front of the train and climbed into the first two coaches behind the engine. Molly boarded the fourth car with Brooks and Asa Lemmon. Brooks called to his chef in the car ahead to serve dinner and then signaled his conductor. Moments later the train pulled away and quickly built up speed.

"By the time we finish eating," Brooks said, "we'll be coming into Wolf Ridge. It will be dark, and we'll switch onto a far siding. You can take your horse out of the stock car and ride back to the livery without attracting attention."

Molly nodded.

Brooks added, "Asa will check into The Montanan. From now on, if you need to get a message to me, send it through him."

"Where will you be?" Molly asked.

"I'll take these men back to Chicago," he replied, "and in a couple of weeks I'll return with the first trainload of prospective farmers." He paused. "In the meantime no one has seen me around here."

Molly understood his strategy. Today he had delivered a strong message to Sam Streeter. The rancher's first reaction would be to strike back. But Brooks would not be in the state, and Sheriff Jenkins could not prove beyond a doubt that the railroad tycoon had led the attack.

In the dining car that evening the men were jubilant while fifty tons of roaring steam engine hurtled them across the high plains toward Wolf Ridge. They devoured big steaks with all the trimmings and lifted shot glasses filled with Kentucky bourbon as they proposed toasts to Preston Brooks. The men might have been returning home from a successful elk or bear hunt.

In the following days the shootings were among the main topics of conversation in Wolf Ridge. The bodies were brought in and identified by Sheriff Jenkins from photographs on wanted posters. All four men were wanted in half a dozen states for crimes ranging from robbery to murder.

The expected outcry from Sam Streeter never came, at least not publicly. While Molly toured shops and stores, as well as saloons and gambling halls off the main street, she got some sense of the public mood. Few people doubted that Preston Brooks had taken the law into his own hands when "unknown gunmen" attacked the Bar S Bar line camp.

Indeed, most townspeople said the outlaws had received their just reward, and the fact that the working cowhands had not been harmed went a long way toward making Brooks a hero in Wolf Ridge.

Asa Lemmon had taken the suite at the end of the hall on the second floor of The Montanan. Molly watched as he opened the homestead locator office on Main Street a few doors down from the hotel. She saw him several times both in the hotel and in the office as she walked past on the boardwalk, but they did not speak. At work he and a clerk were often hunched over maps spread out on a wide table, evidently familiarizing themselves with land that would soon go up for sale.

The sale was preceded by a flurry of handbills delivered to every town along the NA&P rail line.

FREE LAND!

Working for others? Making your boss rich by your labors? Tired of the grind in your office or factory?

GO TO MONTANA!

Be your own boss on your own farm. Make yourself rich by your labors. Get a new start in life.

FREE LAND! FREE LAND!

North American & Pacific right-of-way acreage available now. This is the greatest wheat farming land in the world. For every acre you buy, you will be given one full acre. Free land for a new start in life. Ten per cent down, the rest in easy payments over six years. This is the chance of a lifetime.

FREE LAND! FREE LAND!

Take a free ride on the NA&P to inspect this newly opened farming land. Do not miss out. Free round trip from the NA&P station nearest your home to the HOMESTEAD LOCATOR OFFICE in Wolf Ridge, Montana.

FREE LAND!

The offer of a free ride on the NA&P proved irresistible to hundreds of people within 48 hours. The population of Wolf Ridge swelled as long passenger trains brought men, women, and children eager to see this new land.

On a siding by the depot Preston Brooks brought in a coach filled with farming exhibits, including shocks of wheat from last year's crop. Straw-hatted barkers extolled the virtues of dry-land farming while announcing the sale of another ten-, twenty-, or thirty-acre farm every few minutes. The line of men at the homestead locator office stretched far out into Main Street.

Molly watched as the carnival atmosphere lasted through the week. Special trains came and went. Prospective farmers from many states and a number of families from European countries who spoke little English were taken by train out to farm sites on right-of-way lands. They toured farms that had been established last year and then returned to Wolf Ridge, where they were urged to join the line of buyers at the homestead locator office.

Ranchers and cowhands came to town to see this sight. Their weathered faces lined by frowns, the men sat their saddles and watched the farm folk that now crowded the streets of Wolf Ridge. These people had filled every boarding house and spare room, and now they populated a small tent city on the other side of the railroad tracks.

From the window of the hotel dining room Molly saw a familiar horse and buggy pass by, heading for the depot. It was driven by Sam Streeter. Helene sat erect in the tufted seat beside him, wearing a long linen duster over a large hat secured by a scarf tied under her chin. Molly left half her meal on the plate, and hurried out of the hotel.

She strode along the crowded boardwalk to the depot. Crossing the loading platform, she saw the Streeters entering the farm exhibit car on a siding.

Molly stepped over two sets of tracks, her feet crunching on cinders and gravel. She climbed the metal steps of the car, entering between a shiny plow and a new cook stove. In the aisle ahead stood a dozen or fifteen people looking at the equipment and the photographs on the walls.

Sam Streeter was among them, glowering as he examined samples of last year's wheat, pictures of ready-made homesteader shacks, and banners promising a new life for dry-land farmers in the great state of Montana. Helene stood nearby, not seeing Molly. Her head was tilted downward, as though expecting an explosion. It was not long in coming.

"This is the slickest way to rob folks I ever saw," Sam Streeter said in a loud voice.

Heads turned and a long silence followed his remark. Streeter's gaze darted around the interior of the car and then met the eyes directed at him.

"I've lived in this country almost twenty years," he went on, "and I've seen good, hard-working folks come and go. Most ranched, but some tried to farm. In a wet season they got a crop. That's because we get into a rain cycle once in a great while. Happened last year. Might get rain again this season, too. But I can guarantee you one thing: we won't get three wet years in a row."

Streeter paused while surveying the people in the car. "So all you folks who put your hard-earned money down for a piece of Montana will pull out next year. And you won't have a thing but misery to show for it. Not one damned thing. You know who'll have your money? You know who'll repossess your equipment? You know who'll have your land? Preston Brooks, that's who!"

"Is that gospel, Sam?"

Molly heard the voice from the far end of the railroad car, and then saw the crowd part as a man shouldered his way through them. He was Preston Brooks.

CHAPTER XII

Molly watched as the two men faced one another, eyes meeting and holding in the ensuing silence. Neither man openly displayed anger, but their antagonism was unmistakable.

Molly's gaze went to Helene Streeter. Face upturned now, her eyes were bright with anticipation and a strange delight. Molly saw this at a glance, and in the next instant her attention was captured by Preston Brooks.

"In case you folks don't know this gentleman," he said, turning to address the people who looked on, "he is Sam Streeter, owner of the Bar S Bar Ranch. The Bar S Bar is one of the great cattle ranches of Montana. I've shipped Mr. Streeter's beef to the Chicago stockyards since the day my railroad was completed."

Brooks cast a friendly grin at the glowering Streeter. "Now, as a cattleman, Mr. Streeter can't be expected to know about the latest scientific methods of dry-land farming that we're teaching settlers out here. But as more and more of you make a go of it, he'll learn."

Several men chuckled at this remark.

Streeter's broad face reddened while he stared at his adversary.

"Folks, I don't want your land, I don't want your equipment, and I don't want your money. That's why I'm practically giving the land away, land I paid for a few years ago. No, I want every one of you to make a go of it out here. I want you to make it big." He paused. "And then I want you to ship your grain on my railroad. That way, we'll all be happy."

The people glanced at one another and smiled, nodding their approval.

His face blood red, Sam Streeter turned and strode away. He brushed past Molly as he stomped out of the exhibit car. Helene followed, briefly surprised to see Molly standing by the door, and then went out. Molly heard her light footfalls on the metal steps.

Molly stayed a few minutes while Brooks continued talking in a jovial manner. He skillfully soothed doubts that may have been raised by Streeter, and soberly advised these people to consider carefully before making the decision to buy a farm on the NA&P right-of-way.

"Dry-land farming in this north country is a good life," he said, "but not an easy one. Ask those families who have already made a go of it."

Preston Brooks paused, eyeing his audience with a sense of dramatic timing. "You'll break ground that's never been broken, and you'll put in a crop and every day you'll watch the western sky for the next thunderhead. And after your crop is harvested and sold, you'll brace yourself for a Montana winter. No, this life is not for the fainthearted. It's for strong people, people who are willing to pay the price for a self-sufficient life."

With this challenge — delivered with Bible-pounding intensity — Brooks turned and walked out of the car. As he passed Molly at the door, he winked.

Molly never saw him again. The next day while escorting a trainload of prospective farmers through NA&P land, a rifleman fired from ambush. Before the horrified eyes of dozens of people Preston Brooks fell to the ground, dead, with a bullet through his chest.

The news was delivered to Molly by Asa Lemmon. He came to her in the hotel, jaw quivering as he spoke.

"That goddamned Sam Streeter . . ." Lemmon said. "He's not going to get away with this."

When he was gone Molly sat on the bed in her hotel room, dazed and disbelieving. In her mind's eye she saw Preston Brooks again, remembering the time she had awakened in his private coach, wondering how she had survived the gunshot wound in her chest. She recalled all the other times she had seen him, from the time they had met in the solarium of Mrs. Boatwright's Boarding House to their moment of intimacy when they kissed. And in her mind she again saw his handsome face when he winked at her on his way out of the farm exhibit car.

At last her tears were cried out. Molly's sorrow was replaced by determination. After powdering her face and making herself presentable, she left The Montanan and walked to the train depot. A flag there was at half mast, and a pair of workmen were draping black crepe over a private coach behind the Silver Comet.

Molly entered the depot and crossed the high-ceilinged room to a screened window under the sign that read "Telegrapher." The message she sent to Horace Fenton relayed the news of the railroad tycoon's death, along with a request. She asked for expense money that would allow her to stay in Montana and investigate the murder.

The reply came quickly. Fenton, citing his shock over the death of his friend, wired one thousand dollars to Molly and urged her to bring the killer to justice.

Molly found Sheriff Willard Jenkins in his office. He was leaning down in his swivel chair as she entered, pulling off his boots. Face contorted with the effort, he looked up at her.

"Well, well, Miss Owens," he said, tossing the boot toward its mate, "I've been wondering about you. Any luck in —"

"Sheriff," Molly interrupted, "I'd like to speak to you confidentially about an important matter."

"Why . . . sure," he said slowly. "What is it?"

"The reason I came to Wolf Ridge," she said, "is not the one I told you."

Jenkins' eyebrows raised high on his forehead. "That so," he said half seriously.

Molly pulled an identification badge out of her handbag. "I'm an operative for the Fenton Investigative Agency," she said, handing the badge to him. "I came here to conduct an undercover investigation."

Now he was genuinely amazed. "A Fenton detective?" His gaze went from her to the badge, and back again. "You? A woman? I'll be damned." He stared at her while it soaked in. "Who hired you?"

"Preston Brooks," Molly said.

"What?" he exclaimed.

Molly briefly explained the nature of her investigation without going into many details or revealing names.

"I see," Jenkins said noncommittally. He drew a deep breath. "So that's how Brooks got onto those outlaws using the Bar S Bar line camp."

Molly nodded. "But I hope you'll keep that to yourself, sheriff. I don't want to make trouble for the people I questioned in the course of my investigation." She did not say so, but she was thinking particularly of Helene Streeter.

"I see what you're getting at," he said. He paused as he thought about it. "I don't reckon anyone needs to know about that. You aim to keep your identity secret any longer?"

"No," Molly said.

"And you're going to look into Brooks' killing?" he asked. "Is that your idea?"

She nodded.

"Well, now," he said, leaning back in his chair, "I don't reckon that's a wise thing to do. Me and two deputies are working on the case."

"I won't get in your way," Molly said.

"And I will turn over to you any information or evidence I find."

Jenkins shook his head. "I'd just as soon you stayed clear of this case altogether, Miss Owens. Take some friendly advice for your own good health."

"What do you mean?" she asked.

"Well, for one thing," he said, "folks are not going to take kindly to you when they find out you cooked up that story about hunting for your husband."

"I'm prepared for that," Molly said.

The sheriff shrugged slightly, and came down in his chair. "Maybe so. But there's something else you might not be ready for." He paused. "Whoever gunned down Preston Brooks is likely to come after any detectives on his trail."

Unfazed, Molly said, "You're suggesting the killer is still here."

"Now, I never said that," Jenkins replied. He studied her. "What's your idea — the killer came here just to gun down Brooks? Maybe someone who had a grudge against him?"

"That's possible," Molly said. "Or someone around here hired a killer, one who did the job from ambush and rode out."

The lawman conceded the point with a shrug.

"Do you have a list of suspects?" Molly asked.

"Not yet, we don't," Jenkins said defensively. "We've only just started the investigation. Me and my deputies combed the murder scene without finding a thing, and now we're questioning all the witnesses. There's a slew of them, but I mean to interview every damned one."

"What about Streeter?" Molly asked.

"Don't worry," Jenkins said, "I'll talk to Sam. He'll have to account for his whereabouts. I don't play favorites in a case like this."

"That's good," Molly said, "because this one will get national attention. I should think you'd welcome all the help you can get."

The lawman regarded her. "You know, Miss Owens, there is such a thing as obstruction of justice. Interfering with an officer of the law carries a jail sentence. My best advice to you is to stay clear of this investigation. In fact, you may not even want to stay in town any longer."

"I'm staying, sheriff," Molly said. "It's my right as a citizen."

"True enough," Jenkins said. "I'm just giving you some good advice, that's all."

"You're threatening me," Molly said. She

leaned forward. "I'm here to tell you one thing: one way or another, I'm going to see to it that this murderer is brought in." She turned and strode out of the office.

CHAPTER XIII

Molly left the county sheriff's office, wondering if her strategy of taking the lawman into her confidence had been the right one. Clearly, Jenkins saw her as an adversary, not a friend. She wondered why. Professional pride? Or had Preston Brooks been right when he insisted the sheriff was in the hip pocket of the cattle ranchers?

Too late to change her strategy now, Molly thought as she walked up the boardwalk to the NA&P depot. Actually, she'd had little choice in the matter. She would be unable to maintain her ruse as a wife searching for her husband now that she was actively gathering evidence in a murder case. Sheriff Jenkins would have found out who she was in time, anyway, and that was why she had decided to take the initiative and try to gain his trust and cooperation.

That hadn't worked, but at least the cards were on the table. Hers were, anyway. She had learned very little from the lawman. She was, however, interested in his claim that he and his deputies had combed the scene of the crime without turning up any evidence. That meant that even the killer's hiding place was still unknown.

All the people who had witnessed the murder were still in Wolf Ridge, and Molly spent the rest of the morning seeking them out in the NA&P depot, the homestead locator office, where Asa Lemmon was busy assuring prospective buyers that right-of-way land was still for sale, and two boarding houses off the main street. All of the people Molly spoke to described a scene of panic and chaos after the murder. No one had actually seen the killer, but several men had recognized the deep boom of a rifle that had been fired from a great distance.

Molly returned to The Montanan and changed to her riding clothes. She walked hurriedly to the livery barn wearing a divided riding skirt, a cotton blouse, a scarf knotted around her neck, and a gray Stetson. In her handbag she carried her Colt Lightning Model .38 revolver.

On a saddle horse rented from the livery barn a block and a half away from the hotel Molly left town on the road that paralleled the NA&P tracks. This was the same road Helene Streeter had taken when she'd driven Molly to the Bar S Bar line camp.

Where the road veered away from the tracks and angled up the hill overlooking the homesteaded valley, Molly left it and followed the railroad tracks. Three-quarters of an hour later she reached the scene of the murder.

It was not difficult to locate. On flat ground beside the tracks she saw crumpled handbills, an empty sack of chewing tobacco, and assorted debris amid trampled weeds and grass. Molly reined up and dismounted.

She walked in a widening circle, searching the ground. At first glance the land on this side of the tracks appeared flat. But as Molly walked farther she saw a ravine and a swell of grassy land beyond it.

Stopping, Molly turned and faced the railroad tracks. She tried to visualize the passenger train that had stopped there. The prospective farmers and their wives and children had climbed to the ground. Preston Brooks had walked out here somewhere, facing the crowd and the train. He spoke of this unbroken land and the virtues of farming without irrigation. And then the rifleman's bullet struck him in the back.

Molly turned around. The killer had been out there, somewhere, lying in wait.

Molly walked out to the ravine. She saw horse tracks here, and realized they had been left by the sheriff and his two deputies. The hoofprints went into the sandy bottom of the dry ravine, where the lawmen had evidently searched without finding any clue to the killer's location.

Molly crossed the ravine, angling east as she walked up the swell of grassy land. One witness she had interviewed remarked that Brooks had lurched to his left as he fell forward. That observation gave her an idea. The shot had come at an angle, and now Molly walked in that direction. The killer might have lain in the grass, she thought, beyond the ravine. No horse or boot tracks were out here. If her theory was the right one, Sheriff Jenkins had given up his search for clues too soon.

Molly walked a long way before she looked back toward the railroad tracks and realized she had gone too far. She stopped and turned around. The distance was too great even for a marksman.

Discouraged, she started back. Her instincts, finely honed from other investigations, had told her she was on a fresh trail or close to one. But now she saw no place of concealment. Perhaps the killer had been in that ravine, after all. Perhaps

Sheriff Jenkins had purposely overlooked the killer's trail. . . .

Then she saw something. Off to her right more than fifty yards was a heap of winterkill. Brush and weeds lay amid tufts of greening grass. Molly's pulse quickened as she walked toward it. The line between that spot and the railroad tracks where the crowd had gathered made a greater angle than she had theorized, but now she saw the sense of it.

The dirt behind the dried brush and weeds was disturbed. Molly stopped and studied the signs. Two impressions had been left where the pointed toes of the killer's boots had dug into the ground. The killer had lain prone here, behind the cover of dried weeds and brush.

Molly knelt, sighting straight down the swell of land to the railroad tracks. This was a long shot even for a marksman. But as she visualized the scene of Preston Brooks addressing the crowd she thought she understood the killer's reasoning. From this angle a bullet would not endanger anyone in the crowd if it missed the target.

If the killer wasn't a professional, Molly thought as she straightened up, he certainly was calculating. He came here to murder Preston Brooks and no one else.

Looking around, Molly saw more scrapes in the dirt left by boots. The killer had crawled away, leaving a scene of chaos where his victim had fallen. She followed this faint trail around cactus and over tufts of weeds dried to delicate spires. It led over the swell of ground to a deep ravine 200 yards away. Out of sight of the railroad, the killer had stood and sprinted to the ravine.

When Molly reached it, she descended the steep side, seeing horse droppings down there in the sandy bottom. And her eye was caught by the glint of a brass shell casing.

Molly dropped the shell casing on Sheriff Jenkins' desk. He picked it up and looked at her questioningly.

"That came from the killer's rifle," Molly said.

Eyebrows arching high on his bald head, the lawman said, "That so?"

Molly explained how she had discovered the killer's trail that led her to the ravine. "When he got to his horse, he must have jacked a fresh round into his rifle before he put it into the saddle boot."

"You trailed him?" Jenkins asked.

Molly nodded. "Until the light got too

thin. I'll pick up the trail first thing to-morrow."

Jenkins turned the shell casing over in his stubby fingers. "This is a .44-.40. Plenty of rifles of that caliber around here. A lot of cowhands carry them — hunters, too."

"But how many cowhands or hunters could have made a shot that long?" Molly asked. "It was over three hundred yards."

He looked at her doubtfully. "Miss Owens, are you sure this is all true? Did you really find this out there just like you're claiming?"

Molly felt her face warm. "Sheriff Jenkins, I assure you that everything I've told you is true. I have no reason to lie —"

"You worked for Preston Brooks," he interrupted. "For all I know, you might be trying to frame a rancher for this murder."

"Fenton operatives are not in the business of framing innocent people, sheriff," Molly said. "I'm after the same thing you are — the truth." She paused. "You do want to find this killer, don't you?"

Now Jenkins' face stiffened with anger. "That's right, Miss Owens. But I don't need anyone getting in my way while I'm doing it."

"I brought in evidence, sheriff," Molly

said, gesturing to the shell casing in his hands. "Does that mean I'm in your way?"

A resigned expression crossed his face. In that moment Molly realized that his pride had been injured. She had solved a mystery after he had tried and failed, and he had reacted defensively.

"I can have a deputy ride with you, Miss Owens," he said, "when you pick up that trail in the morning."

Molly heard a conciliatory tone in his voice. But she smiled and shook her head. "I work alone, sheriff."

CHAPTER XIV

After returning the saddle horse to the livery Molly walked back to the main street and followed the boardwalk to The Montanan.

She climbed the stairs to the second floor, sore and tired from a long afternoon in the saddle. Tomorrow would be more of the same, she thought, as she moved down the hall to her room. Unlocking the door, she stepped in and reached for a match to light the lamp on the wall just inside the door. But an instant later, her hand in midair, she froze.

Some scent or sound gave her warning. She plunged her hand into the handbag slung over her shoulder and grasped the pearl grips of her revolver. Drawing the weapon, she leveled it toward a shadowy shape in the far corner of the room.

"You're backlighted," a voice said. "If I'd come here to hurt you, I'd have done it by now."

Molly recognized the voice of Asa Lemmon and lowered the gun. "How did you get in here?"

He held up his hand, and keys jingled. "These belonged to Pres. I'm looking out for his interests now."

"What do you want?" Molly asked.

"We need to have a talk," Lemmon said with a trace of impatience. "Close that door and get a light going."

Molly stood in the doorway for a long moment, not liking his tone of voice. She was tempted to order him out at gunpoint. But then she returned the revolver to her handbag. She might need Asa Lemmon's cooperation in the coming days.

The lamplight that spilled into the far corner of the room showed the narrow-shouldered man slouched in a chair, his small, dark eyes on Molly. Something about his eyes and the way his trimmed sideburns angled across his jaw to join his thin mustache gave him the look of a weasel.

"I do believe everyone in this town is talking about you," Lemmon said, after Molly closed the door.

She cast a questioning glance at him as she took off her Stetson and moved to the end of the brass bed, where she stood facing him.

"A lady investigator is big news out here," he said, straightening up in the chair. "Especially after the way you fooled folks into thinking you were the tearful wife hunting for your lost husband."

"Is that what you came here to tell me?" she asked. The question was met by stern silence, and Molly realized she had failed to conceal her unfriendly mood.

"Look, you don't have to like me," Lemmon said, "but we ought to work together so whoever gunned down Pres will hang from the end of a rope."

He was right, of course, and as Molly stood there she was aware that he was giving her the same speech she had given to Sheriff Jenkins. She took a deep breath and moved to the side of the bed and sat down. She would have to put personal feelings aside.

Molly described her investigation and brought Lemmon up to date on what she had found. She watched his beady eyes while the man listened intently, concluding by telling him that she would pick up the killer's trail first thing in the morning.

"Think that trail will lead you to the Bar S Bar?" he asked.

Molly shrugged.

"The only question in my mind," Lemmon said, "is whether Sam Streeter murdered Pres or hired a sharpshooter to do the job for him."

"Maybe Streeter didn't have anything to

do with it," she said. "I've found no proof yet."

Asa Lemmon snorted. "Now you sound like a damned lawyer."

"As an investigator," Molly said, "I've found it is best to keep an open mind until all the evidence is in."

Lemmon scowled and stood abruptly. "It's one thing to be open-minded, but it's something else to overlook what's obvious." Moving across the room, he added, "Like I say, I don't know how Streeter did it, but I know as sure as I know anything he murdered Pres. And I guarantee you, he'll pay for it."

Molly watched Lemmon fling the door open. He strode out into the hall, leaving the door standing open.

Molly rode out of Wolf Ridge at dawn. She reached the site of Preston Brooks' murder when the sun was a bright orange ball over the eastern horizon. Crossing the grassland to the second ravine beyond the railroad tracks, she picked up the hoofprints in the sandy bottom.

She rode along the bank of the ravine, following the killer's trail for more than a mile. The ravine was deep enough to hide horse and rider, and from the spacing of the tracks Molly saw that the horse had walked. The rider was evidently more concerned with concealment than with a fast escape.

Seeing the hoofprints angle up the far slope, Molly crossed the ravine and followed the tracks across a flat stretch of ground spotted with tufts of new grass. Straight ahead several miles stood the rock-crested ridge Molly had seen from a greater distance the first time she had ridden from town to the Bar S Bar Ranch headquarters. From here the ranch lay far to the north.

By noon the killer's trail had led to the base of that rocky ridge. Molly lost sight of the tracks on rock-strewn ground at the base of the formation, but saw a break in the ridge where the horsebacker must have gone.

The climb was steep. When her horse labored, Molly dismounted and led the animal up the narrow passage that was a crack in the stone. The top, she found, was flat, sloping downward to the south.

Molly walked around the top of the ridge until she found horse droppings. Oats were scattered along the ground. Knowing the killer had left his horse here, Molly walked back to the edge of the ridge, looking down from the high precipice. She had a panoramic view of the land between here and the swell of grassland that concealed the railroad bed several miles away.

Molly thought she understood the killer's reasoning. From this high ground he could readily see if he was pursued. A marksman with a rifle, he must have been confident that if a posse rode after him, he could pick off several from here. The posse would probably turn back, or at least get out of his range. Then the killer could ride to freedom.

But the precaution had been unnecessary, Molly thought. No posse had come in hot pursuit. The killer had gone free.

Where had he gone? Molly searched the ground in a widening circle. She made one discovery. Near the edge of the precipice she found a cigarillo butt. The length of her little finger, it was chewed at the end. She picked it up and put it in her skirt pocket.

Even though this was the first clue she'd found since the shell casing from the killer's rifle, she was growing discouraged. In all likelihood the killer had ridden from here to the Wyoming border, stopping somewhere along the way to pick up his pay where it had been left by previous agreement.

That was the case if she was correct that someone had hired this rifleman. Molly studied the white stone around the spilled oats, and now she saw a scratch mark from a horseshoe. That one led to another, and another.

This faint trail led across the top of the ridge. Molly lost it for a time, but then saw more horse droppings. She became excited. The tracks were not leading to the south. She followed them all the way to another break in the stone formation. The trail clearly led down there, back to the base of the ridge. She got her horse and followed.

Her enthusiasm was quickly dashed. Even though the killer's trail was plain and easy to follow for half a mile after she reached the base of the ridge, she lost it on hard ground. This time she could not pick it up again.

Molly reined up. Now she doubted the theory that Pres had been gunned down by a hired killer who had made his getaway. The killer had simply tried to hide and had ridden to a place where he could see if he was pursued. Determining that he wasn't, he rode back off the ridge to return to his starting point.

Maybe Asa Lemmon had been right, she

thought. Maybe she had been overlooking the obvious. Where she lost the hoofprints, the killer's trail was leading in a northerly direction, back toward the Bar S Bar Ranch.

Molly made a hard ride back to Wolf Ridge. After changing to a dress she sought out Sheriff Jenkins, at last finding the lawman in the saloon district, where he was mediating a confrontation between Lillie and a large group of women in the street. The women held a big white banner with black lettering that read, "Montana Decency League."

"Sheriff, this is a free country," said a woman standing in front of the banner, "and this year we chose to parade right here."

"The hell," Lillie said, her jaw jutting out of folds of fat. "They're here to make trouble for me, sheriff. That's as plain as day. I have a right to conduct my business without this bunch of do-gooders —"

"Ladies, ladies," Jenkins said, raising his hands in the air, "I don't know what the answer to this thing is, but I do know that I'm paid to keep the peace around here."

"Then we can stay!" one of the women shouted.

"You can parade up and down this street

all you want," Jenkins said, "but I'd better warn you. There's a bad element here and I don't have the manpower to guard you."

"We're not afraid!" another well-dressed lady said.

"We'll clean up this cesspool!" shouted one of the women holding the banner.

Lillie glared at Jenkins, then turned to the women in the street. "All right! March out here! See if I care! But I'll tell you one thing. If you try to drive me out of business, I'll put a big sign out here, bigger than that parade banner, with all the names of my clients on it. And you listen to me! You're gonna be mighty surprised at some of those names! You're gonna read some of your own husbands' names on that list!"

"You despicable wretch," said one of the women.

Lillie's hands shot out like claws as she went for the stout woman who said that, but Sheriff Jenkins quickly moved between them.

"Hold it! That's enough!" he shouted. "Now, I told you I'd keep the peace, and I'll do it. If you ladies can't march peaceably, then get on home."

"We're marching!" one of the women said.

But as Molly looked on from the boardwalk across the street, she saw that Lillie's threat had had some effect. The women huddled and then stretched out in a line from one side of the street to the other. They marched the length of the saloon district, then quickly disbanded and headed for Main Street.

"And don't come back!" Lillie shouted after them.

Molly watched as Jenkins spoke to the madam, clearly scolding her. When they parted, Lillie returned to her Victorian- style house, and Jenkins came across the street. When he saw Molly, he veered toward her.

"I wondered how you were going to handle that situation," Molly said.

"Handle it," he said, stepping up onto the boardwalk. "I'd rather handle a bunch of drunks. At least I'd know what to do with them. When the mayor's wife called Lillie a wretch or a witch or whatever she said, I thought there was going to be a slaughter."

"That lady is the wife of the mayor?" Molly asked in surprise.

Jenkins nodded. "Judith Wolcott is tough, but I don't think she could handle a barroom brawler like Lillie." He paused, studying her. "What did you find out there today?"

Molly described the trail she had followed from the deep ravine to the top of the stone ridge, explaining that the killer had not fled for the Wyoming line but had doubled back. She handed the cigarillo butt to him.

"Not much of a clue," he said, turning it over in his hand. He motioned to the saloons on this street. "You'll find plenty of men here smoking these things. But I'll stick it in the evidence envelope with that .44-.40 shell casing you brought in."

"The killer's trail led north when I lost it," Molly said. "If I'd continued in a straight line, I'd have ridden to Bar S Bar land."

Jenkins' expression hardened. "You figure I ought to have Sam Streeter locked up right now, don't you?"

"I didn't say that —" Molly began.

"You and that Asa Lemmon have this thing figured the same way, don't you?" he demanded. "He's threatening to go to the governor if I don't put Sam in jail."

"Hold on, sheriff," Molly said. "If my investigation points to Streeter, then I'll say he should be brought to trial. But right now I don't know who's guilty. I do know that outlaws used the Bar S Bar as a hideout once. Now a killer may be taking refuge there."

"Not with Sam's permission," Jenkins said stubbornly. "I just can't believe Sam would have anything to do with such a thing."

"I plan to give him a chance to deny it," Molly said. "First thing tomorrow."

CHAPTER XV

Molly was met at the door of the Bar S Bar ranchhouse by the uniformed maid, Jane. She invited Molly into the front parlor to wait for "the lady."

Molly sat down on an upholstered settee. Moments later she heard purposeful footsteps descending the stairs. Helene Streeter strode into the parlor, her lips drawn together in a thin line.

"You have a lot of nerve to show your face in my home, Molly Owens," she said. "Or whatever your name is."

Molly stood and faced her. "My name is just what I told you."

"At least you didn't lie about that," Helene said crisply. "And to think I befriended you, helped you . . ."

"You helped me find out the truth," Molly said. "Outlaws were using that line camp —"

"But Sam knew nothing of it," she interrupted. "He only knew saddle tramps occasionally used that cabin."

"I've never accused your husband of wrongdoing," Molly said.

"Oh, no?" Helene asked in a challenging

voice. "You certainly have convinced a lot of people in Wolf Ridge that Sam is running an outlaw ranch. We've put our life's work into this place, and over the years we've earned a good reputation. Now it's ruined because of you, you and those gunmen who attacked the line camp."

She drew a breath. "Now, I suppose you've come here to accuse my Sam of murder. Most folks are ready to believe he's a murderer, aren't they? Because of you, they think the worst of him."

"Helene —"

"It's true!" Helene shrieked. "You know it's true, damn you!"

Molly started to move past her toward the door.

Helene's hand shot out. She grasped Molly above the elbow, squeezing until her nails dug into flesh.

"Let go, Helene," Molly said softly. "I'm leaving. That's what you want, isn't it?"

Enraged, Helene stared into Molly's eyes. "You want to ruin my husband, don't you? You're a lying bitch who's out to ruin my Sam."

"No," Molly said.

"You lied to me before," Helene said. "You're lying now."

Molly met her fierce gaze. "Helene, I

came here to explain why I had to use that disguise. And I came to ask your help."

"Help," Helene repeated with a scowl.

"That's right," Molly said. "You may be the one person who can help prove your husband's innocence."

Helene blinked. "What?"

"I feel bad that I misled you about my identity, Helene," Molly said. "But it was part of my job, and I had to do it in order to arrive at the truth. Now I'm searching for Preston Brooks' murderer, and I think you can help me."

Helene released Molly's arm and shook her head.

"But if you'll help me —" Molly began.

Helene shook her head again, stepping back. "I know what you're saying: If my husband is innocent, your investigation will prove it."

"That's right," Molly said.

"But if Sam ever found out I'd spoken to you, much less helped you in any way, he'd. . . ." She groped for words. "Well, I don't know what he'd do. He despises you, Molly."

"Do you?" Molly asked.

"I . . . I'm just awful mad," she replied. She exhaled. "Oh, I don't know. Maybe Sam's looking at it all wrong."

"I want us to be friends," Molly said.

Helene said nothing.

Molly met her gaze for a long moment and moved toward the door.

Helene followed. "Have you investigated Preston Brooks' background?"

Surprised by the challenging tone in her voice, Molly stopped in the entryway and faced the ranch-woman. "What do you mean?"

"Just what I said," Helene said, folding her arms under her small breasts. "You present yourself as being fairminded. I should think you'd want to investigate Preston Brooks as carefully as you're investigating my husband." She paused. "You should look into his . . . affairs."

"Affairs?" Molly said.

"That's right," Helene said with a trace of smugness. "Ask around town. You might learn a few things about the famous Preston Brooks."

"Sounds like I should start by asking you," Molly said.

"I don't spread gossip," Helene said. She added, "Everyone in Wolf Ridge knows the truth about him."

"If it's the truth," Molly said, "I'd like to hear it."

"Are you certain you want to hear the

unvarnished truth about the man you worked for?" Helene asked.

Molly nodded, growing impatient with this cat-and-mouse game.

"A seventeen-year-old girl left town on short notice," Helene said. "She left on a private coach, all expenses paid. Everyone knows she went to a home for unwed mothers in Chicago. Now, you put two and two together."

"Why don't you just tell me the whole story," Molly said.

"It's no story," Helene said. "I know the girl's parents. Her mother was a member of the Decency League before this happened."

"What's her name?" Molly asked.

"I'll only tell you this much," Helene said. "That pregnant girl is the daughter of a schoolteacher in town." She added, "So, you see, Molly, Preston Brooks had other enemies, too."

On the way back to Wolf Ridge Molly reconsidered her investigation. While she disliked Helene's manner of spreading gossip, she had to admit that she had overlooked an important point in the investigation. Preston Brooks had a strong personality. He was a man who took action without regard to the enemies he might make.

Now that Molly suspected the murderer was not an outsider, the logical next step was to conduct interviews in town. Sam Streeter was not going anywhere. If other enemies of Brooks' were in Wolf Ridge, now was the time to find them.

Of the three teachers in Wolf Ridge School, one was a man. The others were women, and by local regulation they were single. The schoolmarm who married was out of a job.

The man's name, Molly learned from the waitress who brought her a late breakfast in the hotel dining room, was John Copeland. He taught the upper grades in addition to acting as principal of the whitewashed frame schoolhouse a block west of Main Street.

After lingering over a second cup of coffee, Molly left The Montanan. She had slept a hard, dreamless sleep last night, awakened at dawn, and rolled over in bed to sleep for another two hours. After a hot soak in the bathroom at the end of the hall, she had dressed and come downstairs for breakfast.

Now Molly crossed Main Street and walked down a side street to the newest residential section of town. Freshly painted houses were here, decorated with lacey gingerbread and marked off by wrought iron or white picket fences. In several backyards Molly saw the morning's wash hanging on the line. Geraniums and pansies bloomed along walks and in window flower boxes, and in one curtained bay window in a corner house Molly was watched by a toddler whose golden hair was highlighted by morning sunshine.

The shouts of boys and the shrieks of girls grew louder as Molly rounded the corner and crossed the street to the school. In the playground a baseball game was in progress, and Molly saw a settling cloud of dust where a boy in short pants had just slid into home plate. From the steps of the schoolhouse a man watched impassively.

Molly followed the walk past the flagpole to the front door where the man stood. His gaze swung to her, and as Molly drew closer he seemed to stiffen slightly.

"I wondered when you'd get around to me," he said.

Molly stopped at the bottom of the stairs and looked up at him. Her mental image of a schoolteacher did not fit him. He was tanned in the face and broad shouldered, and his sleeves were rolled past the elbows of his heavily muscled arms.

"You know me?" Molly asked.

He gave her a curt nod as another chorus of cheers erupted on the playground. "I know nearly everyone in town by sight, and you match the description of the blonde woman most folks are talking about."

"Are you Mr. Copeland?" she asked.

"That's right, Miss Owen," he replied as though the question was a needless formality.

"Owens," Molly said with a smile. She mounted the steps and held out her hand to shake. "My name is Molly Owens."

After hesitating, Copeland shook hands with her.

"I'd like to talk to you," Molly said. "In private."

He pursed his lips and glanced out at the baseball game. "All right, come in."

Copeland turned and pulled the door open. Molly stepped into a hallway. Four classrooms, two on either side, opened into this hall. At the end was a door with large black lettering across it: "Principal."

Copeland did not speak until they were inside his office and the door was shut. The room was bare and had the appearance of being little used. A desk and two straight-backed chairs were the only furnishings, along with a paddle standing against the far wall.

"Well, I suppose you've heard all about Celia," he said. "Damn few secrets in this town."

"Celia's your daughter?" Molly asked.

Copeland nodded.

"I'd like to hear about her from you," she said.

He exhaled loudly, folding his thick arms over his chest. "This is an exercise in futility, isn't it? I've said more than once that I'd like to see a headstone with Preston Brooks' name on it. Now you come around here, looking for someone to pin a murder on."

"I'm not here to pin a murder charge on an innocent man," Molly said.

Copeland's mouth quivered. "Well, I may be guilty of celebrating Brooks' death, but I'm not guilty of murdering him." Tears welled in his eyes.

Molly watched as he wiped a big hand across his face. He backed against his desk and leaned on it.

"Where were you that day?" Molly asked. "Here?"

Coleman shifted his feet uncomfortably. "Not in the morning. I was ill." He added, "My wife can corroborate that, though I don't suppose her testimony would be considered in court."

"Let's not get ahead of ourselves," Molly said. "Right now I'm just trying to get some basic facts straight in my mind. Did you teach at all that day?"

"Oh yes," he replied. "I came in at noon. I taught the remainder of the day and left here about four."

"There must be plenty of witnesses who can corroborate that," Molly said with a smile.

He nodded and said ruefully, "A room full of fifth and sixth graders who aren't likely to forget that afternoon. I gave them a surprise exam, and none of them did well — not even my best students."

"Was Celia a good student?" Molly asked.

Copeland was surprised by the question. He eyed Molly. "She did well when she put her mind to it. Celia was . . . is a restless girl. Why do you ask?"

"I'd like to know more about her," Molly said. "I'd like to know exactly what happened between her and Preston Brooks."

"It's simple enough," Copeland said with a pained expression. "Brooks was a famous, handsome man with expensive tastes — exotic, you might say. For his entertainment, he found the most beautiful young woman in this town and seduced her. When she discovered she was pregnant, Brooks offered her money. That's when Celia came to her mother, and they both came to me — in tears. Celia couldn't . . ." His voice faltered. "Celia could not understand why the man she loved would not marry her."

Footsteps thundered in the hall as students came in from recess. Copeland's head snapped up at the sound, and then he looked at Molly.

"I presume you'll repeat all this to Sheriff Jenkins," he said, "and that I may expect a visit from him next."

Molly said, "I'm going to tell the sheriff why I think you're innocent."

"What?" he said in amazement.

"According to my investigation, Mr. Copeland," Molly said, "you didn't have time to shoot Preston Brooks and get back to this schoolhouse by noon."

He straightened up as though a weight had been lifted from his shoulders. Glancing toward the door, he said, "I really must go to my class."

Molly held out her hand to shake. "I'd like to talk to you again sometime about your daughter — painful as it may be to you."

Copeland nodded. "All right." He managed a smile. "It's been good talking to you, Miss Owens. You don't know how good."

CHAPTER XVI

There were at least two sides to every story, Molly thought, while she walked back to Main Street, and she wondered exactly what people were saying behind John Copeland's back in this town. Was Celia really the innocent victim that her father portrayed her to be?

Molly no longer considered him a suspect, even though Copeland lived with a sense of rage directed toward Preston Brooks. She had discovered, too, that he lived with a fear that one day he would be charged with murder.

No, Molly thought, the timing was too far off. Preston Brooks had been gunned down late in the morning. The assassin's trail led farther away from town. It would have been impossible for Copeland to have covered that distance in time to arrive at the schoolhouse by noon.

Molly found her thoughts returning to Celia. Perhaps the reason was that they had both shared a strong attraction to Preston Brooks. But also Molly sensed she was an important link in the case. Molly briefly considered the idea of taking the train back to Chicago to question her.

But as she reached Main Street, she gave up the idea. She needed to keep the investigation moving here. She knew where to find the best source of information in a "delicate matter" like this one, and now after she waited for a Concord stagecoach to pass by, she crossed the street and headed for Lillie's place.

If Lillie had a last name, Molly had never heard it. From the day she had first encountered the fat woman in the county sheriff's office to her tours of the saloon district while she posed as a wife hunting for her lost husband, Molly had heard dozens of men refer to "Lillie's place." And the day before yesterday she had stood across the street from the Victorian mansion during the confrontation between the madam and the ladies of the Decency League.

Set at the far end of the saloon district amid a hodgepodge of log cabins and tar-paper shacks, the brothel was two stories of Victorian elegance. Bay windows and an enclosed porch graced the front of Lillie's place, and upstairs Molly noted the tall, narrow windows where heavy curtains were drawn. A wrought-iron fence, like a row of upturned spears, enclosed the property, which included a carriage house and servants' quarters out back.

Molly walked to the iron gate and worked the latch. The gate opened soundlessly on oiled hinges. She followed the walk to the porch and climbed the half-dozen steps to an outsized door. Turning the brass handle of the doorbell, she heard it ring softly inside. Half a minute later the door opened.

A burly man whose ample muscles were defined by tight clothes stood in the doorway. His hair was slicked down like a coat of paint, and his lips were unusually fat. They curved into a smile as he gave Molly a critical once-over, like a stockman examining beef on the hoof with a practiced eye.

"I'm here to see Lillie," Molly said.

He nodded once and stepped back, motioning for her to enter. Molly moved into a carpeted hallway. To her left a staircase curved up to the second floor. Down the hall a short distance on the right was an arched doorway. The muscular man stopped there and in a surprisingly feminine voice told Molly to step inside and wait.

Her feet cushioned by a thick Persian carpet, Molly went into a lavishly furnished parlor. Settees and high-backed chairs were crowded into this room. Along the far wall was a black marble fireplace.

Molly saw a painting of a reclining nude hanging over the mantle. Plump with rosebud nipples capping her huge breasts, one foot was folded behind the knee of an outstretched leg, and where her thighs came together was a cloud of dark hair. The nude seemed to peer sleepily into this room, perhaps looking at the elaborately carved back bar across the way, where dozens of champagne goblets lined the shelves in front of a mirror.

"What can I do for you, honey?"

Startled, Molly quickly turned around. The fat woman had entered the room and silently moved behind her.

Lillie wore a loose, wide-sleeved robe of red silk with a sash tied around her thick middle, and now she smiled. "If you're looking for work —"

"I'm not," Molly said. "My name is Molly Owens, and I'm looking for some information."

Smile fading, Lillie said, "I run a private business here, miss — very private. If I was to tattle . . ." Her voice trailed off as recognition came into her eyes. "Wait . . . you must be that blonde woman I've heard about. A Fenton detective, aren't you?"

Molly nodded. "I'm looking for information about —"

"Get out," Lillie said. Over her shoulder, she called, "Herman!"

The muscular man who had met Molly at the door eased into the room. "Yes, Miss Lillie?" he said in his womanly voice.

"This lady is leaving the premises," Lillie said. "See her to the door."

"Yes, ma'am," Herman said, moving toward Molly. "Come along now."

Molly held up her hand. "Please hear me out. I just have a few questions about —"

Herman closed the distance between them. He grasped Molly's arm, his powerful grip squeezing like a vise. "I said, come along now, dearie."

"Herman," Molly said, "I'm not quite ready to leave yet. Let go of me."

The challenge brought a grin to his thick lips. He gave her a yank, pulling her toward him.

Molly yielded until her opponent relaxed, thinking his point was made. His strength was obviously superior, and if he chose to he could lift Molly off the floor and carry her out of the room under one arm.

Molly half turned as Herman's grip relaxed. Out of the corner of her eye she saw him smile broadly. Dominating her gave him pleasure. In the next instant she raised her arm in front of her, bent at the elbow, and drove it straight back with all of her weight and strength behind it. The point of her elbow caught Herman's thick neck at the Adam's apple.

Herman's eyes bulged. He gasped hoarsely, his face turning red. He lunged for Molly, lashing out with his right fist.

Molly sidestepped the punch. She quickly shifted her weight to one foot, and kicked with the other. The point of her high button shoe struck Herman squarely in the bulge at the crotch of his tight trousers.

He cried out sharply, then his face went slack. He sank to his knees and slowly toppled forward, landing face first on the thick carpet.

Molly turned to the wide-eyed Lillie and asked, "Can we talk now?"

The fat woman could not pull her gaze away from the fallen Herman. "How did you do that?"

"I have a few questions to ask you," Molly said, "and then I'll leave."

Lillie swallowed and at last looked at her. "Questions? About what?"

"About a young woman named Celia Copeland," Molly said.

As though coming out of a daze, Lillie said, "I don't know anything about her."

Molly smiled. "If I found myself in her predicament, I'd come to you for advice. Did Celia?"

"No," Lillie said. Obviously complimented, her expression warmed as she studied Molly.

"Then Preston Brooks must have come to you," Molly said.

"What if he did?" Lillie asked, suspicion returning to her face. "Just what're you out to prove?"

"I'm trying to identify his murderer," Molly said. "You can help me by telling me all you know about Celia Copeland."

On the floor Herman moaned. He rolled his head to one side and tried to get up, but then slumped back down on the carpet, groaning.

"Damn, I can't get over the way you dropped him," Lillie said, shaking her head as she looked down at him. "Herman has whipped some big, mean men who've raised hell in my place, and you walk in here and drop him like a tree."

Molly asked, "Did you know Celia?"

Lillie blinked and turned her attention

to Molly. "Sure, I know the girl. Everybody's seen her around town, swinging that butt of hers like she was the Queen of Sheba. Oh, she's a looker."

"Other men must have been interested in her," Molly said.

"Every man who saw her was interested," Lillie said, grinning. She paused. "Look, if you have some idea Preston Brooks isn't the man who got her pregnant, forget that. He never doubted it. He told me so himself." She added, "Pres and me, we were pretty close."

Molly heard the note of pride in her voice. "But someone else might have been angry enough to kill him — another man."

"Oh, I see what you're getting at," Lillie said. "A love triangle." She thought a moment and shook her head. "No, I don't think so. I happen to know Celia set her sights for Preston Brooks. Every time he was in town, she trailed after him. She ached for him, let me tell you. That snippy girl even came to my door one morning and asked me to fix things so Pres would find her here, ready for him. You can bet I tossed her out in a hurry. I've got enough trouble in this town of do-gooders without that kind of trouble."

"I'd like the address of the place you recommended to Pres," Molly said. "It's in Chicago, isn't it?"

"Close by," Lillie said with a nod. She regarded Molly and shrugged. "What the hell, everything's legal about it. I'll give it to you."

"Thanks," Molly said. On the floor Herman moaned again.

"You've got a way about you," Lillie said to her, "a way like I've never seen before in a proper lady. You don't take any gaff. And, by god, I like that."

Molly walked through the quiet saloon district back to Main Street, glad that she had heard Lillie's version of the story. Celia Copeland sounded like a lovestruck young woman who had finally gotten her way with the man of her dreams. The dream had become a nightmare when Brooks had evidently refused to marry her, and Celia was left with no choice but to accept his money. In her wake, her family suffered embarrassment and humiliation over the affair.

Molly went to the homestead locator office. She found Asa Lemmon and a clerk recording land quadrants in a big logbook. The clerk, a pale young man wearing a green eyeshade and sleeve garters, looked up and stared as Molly came through the door.

Lemmon cleared his throat. "George, why don't you go get yourself a cup of coffee?"

His head snapped around. "Sure, Asa." He quickly capped his pen and set it down on the logbook. Taking the eyeshade off his head, he climbed off the stool and moved past Molly to the door.

After the clerk had gone, Lemmon said, "How come Sam Streeter isn't behind bars?"

"Because there's no proof he's guilty," Molly said.

"Your job is to find the proof," he said.

Molly shook her head. "My job is to gather evidence that will lead to the killer."

"You can be sure of one thing," Lemmon said, pursing his lips, "Sam Streeter is laughing at us right now."

"I'm not so sure of that," Molly said. "You told me yourself that the sale of NA&P right-of-way land will go on. More farmers will come out here this year and next year."

"What're you getting at?" he asked.

"Motive," Molly said. "What did Streeter have to gain by murdering Preston Brooks?"

"Oh, hell," Lemmon said impatiently. "Streeter hated Pres. You know that. And you know what kind of man Pres was.

Without him, the NA&P won't be the powerful company that it was. Farmers may still come out here, but they won't be inspired by the driving enthusiasm of Pres. He was one of a kind."

Lemmon had a point there, Molly had to admit. Without Brooks the North American & Pacific Railroad might flounder. At the very least his vision of bringing thousands of farmers to this part of Montana would be unfulfilled. But still she wondered if that was a strong enough motive to make Streeter commit murder or even hire a local man to do the job.

"What will happen to the NA&P now?" Molly asked.

"Everything will go on as before," Lemmon replied automatically. "Freight is on schedule, and we're selling farm acreage on the right-of-way."

"I know that's what you're telling everyone," Molly said, "but I'm asking you. What will happen in the long run?"

Lemmon replied with a shrug. "We may be bought out by a competitor. Union Pacific has its eye on this line, I've heard. Anyhow, things will go on as before." Then Lemmon said, "Now tell me what you've been doing."

Molly gave him a brief account of her investigation without revealing many details. By his expression she clearly sensed that the Celia Copeland affair was not news to him. She asked a few questions about it, but he replied vaguely. When pressed, he commented that the young woman was being taken care of, very well taken care of in fact, and would say no more.

Molly left the office and angled across Main to the sheriff's office. The door was locked.

Molly followed the boardwalk on to the depot. At the telegraph office she wired a report to Horace Fenton. She also relayed the address of the home for unwed mothers and asked that a Chicago operative be dispatched to interview Celia Copeland.

Returning to The Montanan, Molly climbed the wide staircase to her room. She went in and found that a note had been slipped under the door.

Molly picked up the scrap of paper and unfolded it, seeing words crudely lettered with a blunt pencil:

You want to find out about the Brooks killing meet me on the railroad tracks east of town 8:00 tonight. Come alone or no deal.

CHAPTER XVII

After supper in the hotel dining room, Molly changed to her riding outfit and walked to the livery barn. She rented a saddle horse from a liveryman who had a questioning look on his face but not enough nerve to ask where she planned to go at that time of day.

Molly rode out of Wolf Ridge along the railroad bed. A half moon was high in the sky, casting pale light on the ground. Thickets and tufts of weeds made deep shadows. The top surface of the railroad tracks, worn by the steel wheels of trains, gleamed in the moonlight.

The buildings of town left behind, Molly reined up and dismounted. She had misgivings about this night meeting. It was risky. But with no other leads to follow, she had decided to take a chance. Under her light jacket the Colt .38 rode in her shoulder holster, and her two-shot derringer was strapped to her thigh.

Molly walked beside the horse, using him for protection. If the note that brought her here was from a killer who intended to lure her out of town, he would not have an easy target.

Half a mile farther, the horse suddenly tossed his head and pranced. Molly gripped the reins and held him. She peered into night, trying to see into moonlit shadows. A chill ran up her spine, and she made an intuitive decision.

Molly grasped the saddle horn and thrust her boot into the stirrup. She would ride back to town.

A whispering sound in the air gave warning too late. The loop that settled over her shoulders tightened before she could duck out of it, or reach for her gun. She was yanked off the horse. She hit the graveled roadbed, hard.

Molly struggled in vain as her horse trotted away. The lariat held taut no matter how she turned or where she rolled. Then she heard footfalls pounding toward her.

Against the starry sky Molly saw the figure of a man. He wore a wide-brimmed hat with a round crown. The brim kept his face in night shadows. He knelt over her, and rolled her on her side. Pulling her wrists behind her back, he quickly bound them with a short length of rope.

The man's hands swept over her body. They lingered on her breasts, and squeezed. Then one hand plunged inside her jacket. With a triumphant grunt, he drew out her revolver.

"Sneak gun," he said in a low voice. Standing, he went after her horse.

That voice was vaguely familiar, but Molly could not place it. She turned her head, watching him return with her horse. He whistled to his own horse and shook the lariat loose from her shoulders.

Molly now realized the lariat was tied to the saddle horn of a cutting horse. No wonder she had not been able to get free. That animal was well trained to back up every time the rope slackened.

The man coiled the rope and then bent down and lifted Molly up. He put her into the saddle of her horse. Taking the reins, he led her to his horse. He tossed the coiled rope over the horn, and swung up.

"We're going for a night ride, lady, a long one." He laughed and added, "I told you we'd meet again."

At that moment Molly recognized his voice. Her captor was Buster Welch.

The moon was down by the time the Bar S Bar foreman reached his destination. In the darkness Molly had lost track of time and distance. Riding with her hands bound behind her back made it difficult for her to keep her balance, and several times she nearly fell out of the saddle when the horse dropped into a ravine or climbed a slope.

The boxy shape of a low cabin loomed in the starlight. Buster Welch spoke to his horse, and the animal halted. He threw a leg over the saddle and slid to the ground.

Molly watched as he entered the cabin. Moments later a match flared, and light streamed out of the doorway when he lit a lantern in there.

Hatless now, Welch came out and strode purposefully to Molly's horse. Grasping her around the waist, he lifted her off the saddle and carried her over his shoulder into the cabin. He bent forward and dropped her onto a narrow bunk against the wall.

Molly lay on her back and looked up at his grinning face.

"You and me, we're going to have us a good time, a real good time — soon as I tend the horses."

She watched him leave, and then struggled against the rope that bound her wrists. She got nowhere. The knot was well tied, one that Welch had probably used hundreds of times to secure the kicking hooves of calves while they were branded with a hot iron.

Buster Welch soon returned, carrying his

saddlebags and Winchester rifle. He set his gear down by the door, kicked it shut, and moved silently across the dirt floor to the bunk.

Molly saw him draw a Barlow knife out of his trouser pocket. He opened the blade. He reached behind her and cut the rope in a few smooth sawing motions.

Molly's arms ached as she brought her numb hands in front of her. She rubbed them together, seeing where the skin on her wrists had been rubbed raw by the rope. She slowly sat up, watching Welch.

"Don't get any fool ideas," he said, waving the knife in front of her face. "I don't want to hurt you, but I will if I have to."

"What do you want?" Molly asked.

"You know what I want," he said, his eyes passing over her body. "Peel off your clothes."

"Buster, you killed Preston Brooks, didn't you?" Molly asked.

"Shut up," he said, "and get on with it. I've waited a long time, and I'm gonna show you what a real man can do —"

Molly gestured to the rifle standing against the wall by the cabin door. "Is that the gun you used to kill him? That was a long shot, Buster. I bet you're real proud of it."

"Damn it, woman!" he shouted. "Shut your mouth and strip!" He thrust the knife at her, the point of the blade slicing through her blouse. A droplet of blood appeared there.

"You just made a big mistake, Buster," Molly said.

"Don't make me cut you," he said. He smiled as she crossed her right leg, and reached up to her thigh. "Now, that's more like it. Pull that skirt off —"

Molly's fingers closed around the handle of the derringer. She jerked it out from under her riding skirt, took quick aim at Welch's knife hand, and pulled the trigger. The derringer went off with a loud *pop*.

Welch's hand jerked back as though he had touched a stove top. He howled in pain. The Barlow flipped end over end to the dirt floor.

He grasped the wrist of his wounded hand. "You . . . you shot me," he said, staring in disbelief at the blood dripping from the side of his hand. The bullet had passed through, exiting near the heel of his palm.

Molly stood, aiming the derringer squarely at him. "You look a bit pale, Buster. Better sit down on that bunk."

Pulling his gaze away from his hand, he stared at her.

"Sit down," she said again.

Welch did as he was told. Molly kicked the Barlow knife away and went to the cabin door. Keeping the derringer trained on him, she opened his saddlebags with her free hand. Inside she found her Colt .38.

After holstering the derringer and covering Welch with her revolver, Molly took a closer look at the rifle. It was a short-barreled saddle gun, and probably did not have the range to make the long shot that had felled Preston Brooks.

Molly lifted the rifle and tilted it toward the lantern. She read the numbers engraved on the barrel near the breech. The caliber was .30-.30.

In a way she felt disappointed. If Buster Welch had murdered Brooks, he had not used this rifle. And he did not impress her as a man with enough cunning to perform a killing with one rifle and then discard it for another.

"Whose idea was it to bring me out here, Buster?" Molly asked, leaning the rifle against the wall.

Welch glared at her, still holding his wounded hand in his lap.

"You can tell me," Molly said, "or you

can tell Sheriff Jenkins." She added, "Tell me, and maybe we can work something out."

"Work what out?" he asked dully.

"You're looking at a jail term if I take you in," Molly said. "Cooperate with me, and maybe we can forget this thing ever happened."

"What do you mean, cooperate?" he asked.

"Answer my questions," Molly said. "You can start off by telling me how you cooked up this idea to kidnap me and rape me."

Welch stared at her, grim-faced.

After a long moment Molly said, "All right, then, you can tell it to a judge and jury in Wolf Ridge. You've kidnapped me and attacked me. I will press charges against you, Buster."

"Now, hold on," he said. "Let me think."

"We're riding out of here," Molly said. "Don't stall for time."

"I'm not stalling," he said. He lowered his gaze and whispered, "Damn. I never should have . . ."

"What?" Molly asked. "I can't hear you."

Looking down at the dirt floor, he said aloud, "When Streeter finds out . . . no telling what he'll do. . . ."

"Right now, that's the least of your troubles," Molly said. "Sam Streeter talked you into this scheme, didn't he?"

"I guess you could say that," he replied.

"I don't want any guesses, Buster," Molly said. "I want the truth — all of it. Otherwise, you're going to jail."

"Streeter . . . he said I could have . . . could have my fun with you." Welch took a breath. "He said we had to run you out of Montana . . . figured if I threw a scare into you . . ."

"It was supposed to be more than a scare, wasn't it, Buster?" Molly demanded. "You were going to rape me, and then what?"

"I was supposed to . . ." His voice broke off. "I was supposed to load you on your horse in the morning and take you south . . . to the state line."

"Dead or alive?" Molly asked.

Welch's head jerked up. He looked at her in alarm. "Alive, I swear. I was supposed to put the fear into you, not kill you."

"For that I can thank Sam Streeter," Molly said, with a faint smile. She thought a moment. "And I believe I will."

"What . . . what're you talking about?" Welch asked.

"How far is the home ranch from here?" she asked.

"Five, six hours' ride," he replied slowly. "Just what do you figure on doing?"

"We're going to pay your boss a visit," Molly said.

"Oh, no," Welch said positively, "I'm not going there with you . . . like this?"

"Buster," Molly said, leveling her revolver at him, "I'm not asking you. I'm telling you. At daybreak we're riding. And you're going to lead the way to the Bar S Bar headquarters."

CHAPTER XVIII

At the first light of day Molly rode behind Buster Welch as he headed north for the home ranch. The man rode with his head bowed slightly, shoulders slumped. His injured right hand was bandaged with a blue bandana neckerchief Molly had found in his saddlebags.

Last night she had bound him hand and foot, and she slept until daybreak. Now as she looked at the ranch foreman she almost felt sorry for him. His strutting cockiness was gone, replaced by fear. Welch was clearly dreading the prospect of admitting to Streeter that he had failed to do the job, and worse, that he had been overpowered by a woman.

Molly glanced back at the cabin. Welch had told her over a breakfast of hard biscuits and a can of beans from his saddlebags that the log cabin was an old Bar S Bar line camp, unused since the two cabins and corral had been built where Molly had discovered the train robbers.

The ride over low, grassy hills and through shallow ravines was silent except for the creak of saddle leather and the sounds of laboring horses. They stopped only to rest the horses and to drink from their canteens.

The sun climbed up the eastern sky, and by the time it shone brightly overhead Molly heard a distant clanging. She recognized the sound of a blacksmith's hammer striking metal on an anvil. The *clang clang clang* carried across the distance at a regular beat, like a mighty clock. The horses, sensing stalls and nosebags filled with oats ahead, picked up the pace.

Coming over a grassy swell of land, Molly saw the outbuildings and stately ranch house ahead. The scene was peaceful and ordered with all the buildings and corrals in good repair, firewood neatly stacked, and the pastures beyond the barn dotted with haystacks. The shape and color of them reminded Molly of loaves of bread. In fenced pastures she saw Streeter's purebred bulls and his Percheron and Arabian horses.

Helene Streeter evidently saw them coming, for she stepped out of the house, hesitating as she came down the walk. She watched as Molly rode beside Buster Welch to the gate in the picket fence.

"Is your husband here?" Molly asked her, reining up.

Helene shook her head. She looked at

the ranch foreman, and back to Molly again. "He's out with some of the men, but he should be in for dinner soon." She paused, now seeing Buster Welch's bandaged hand. "What on earth is going on?"

Molly dismounted. She explained what happened to her last night. Helene listened in shocked silence, glancing up at Welch who sat his saddle with a dejected look on his face.

"I don't believe it," Helene said when Molly finished.

"It's true," Molly said. "I have the note to prove it, along with a couple of bruises and a small knife wound from your ranch foreman."

"I mean, I don't believe my husband had anything to do with this," she said. "I don't believe that for a minute."

"I only know what Buster told me," Molly said. "I'd like to hear your husband's side of it."

Helene planted her hands on her hips and glared at the Bar S Bar foreman. "What's this about?"

Looking downward, Welch shook his head slowly. He did not reply.

"You've got plenty of explaining to do," Helene went on, "if you want to continue working here."

Now he looked at her. "Lady, I'm ready to pack my war bag and ride out — today."

"You'll have that chance later on, Buster," Molly said. "Right now you're going to wait here. Climb down."

When Welch hesitated, acting as though he might spur his horse, Molly drew her revolver. She repeated the command. Helene gasped and drew back, watching fearfully.

Welch did as he was told, and Molly marched him to a patch of shade. He knelt there and rolled a smoke. Out of the corner of her eye Molly saw Helene retreat into the house. Three-quarters of an hour later the sounds of drumming hoofbeats brought her outside. She went to the picket fence and stood there, shielding her eyes.

Molly looked to the west, too, seeing Sam Streeter ride over the hill on his cream-colored Arabian. He led half a dozen cowhands to the corral adjoining the largest barn. Streeter turned his mount over to one of his men, and headed for the house. Helene called to him.

Streeter altered course and came to the picket fence. His stride stiffened when he saw Molly. Next his gaze went to Buster Welch.

"What the hell —"

"Your foreman needed an escort home," Molly said to the rancher, "so I brought him."

Welch sheepishly got to his feet, holding his injured hand.

"Goddamn it, Buster," Streeter said.

"Sam, what's this all about?" Helene asked. "Molly told me some horrible things that he did to her and claims you ordered him to . . . hurt her."

"I don't know what she's talking about," Streeter said.

Molly stepped forward. "Are you calling your foreman a liar?"

"Mr. Streeter —" Buster began.

"Shut up," Streeter said.

"You sent Buster after me," Molly said. "You told him to rape me and run me out of the state. Now, are you going to stand there and tell me that isn't true?"

Streeter glared at Welch and lowered his gaze.

"Sam," Helene whispered. "Oh, no, Sam."

"I never meant it that way," he said to her. "I wanted her scared off, that's all." He raised his hands plaintively. "She's aiming to pin that Brooks killing on me. That's the only reason she's still around here. She's gathering up witnesses, a bunch of liars who'll put a noose around my neck. In town that Asa Lemmon fella is bragging about it, saying he'll build the gallows himself."

"If you're innocent," Molly said, "you have nothing to fear from me."

"The hell," Streeter said, swinging around to face her. "You'll concoct a few shreds of evidence, get testimony from people who've taken a dislike to me over the years, and then some high-priced lawyer from the NA&P will do the rest. I'll hang because of you!"

Behind his anger Molly saw fear. He lived with it much the same way John Coleman had lived with the ever-present cold fear that the law was coming for him.

"I don't concoct facts, Mr. Streeter," Molly said. "I'm a trained investigator, and I'm gathering evidence —"

Streeter swore again. He turned away, strode to the picket fence, and threw the gate open. He went into his stone house without looking back.

"Molly," Helene said in a subdued voice, "I'm so ashamed. I . . . I'd better go after him."

Molly watched her pass through the gate and go up the walk to the door. She turned to Buster Welch.

"That's all I wanted from you, Buster," she said.

"You ain't going to press charges against me?" he asked.

Molly shook her head. "We made our deal. I'll stick to my part of it."

Welch moved past her and went to his horse. He took the reins and led the animal away, heading for the horse corral.

Molly debated about what she should do next, and decided to take a chance. She opened the picket gate and went to the front door of the house. Turning the handle, she opened it and stepped into the entryway.

No one was there. Easing the door shut, she stood still, listening. Presently she heard sobbing and the subdued voice of Sam Streeter. He and Helene were upstairs.

Molly moved quickly down the hallway to the door that opened into Streeter's office. She had spotted it when Streeter had brought Welch in here during her first visit.

The door was unlocked. Molly went in, stepping on a bear rug thrown over the polished hardwood floor. She looked around at the masculine furnishings. A large rolltop desk dominated the room. On the wall over it was a surveyor's map showing the Bar S Bar terrain and boundaries. On the other walls were mounted heads of a grizzly bear, a bull elk, and two buck deer with large antlers. Molly closed the door until the latch touched the jamb and crossed the room to the desk.

It was unlocked. She slid the rolltop back and saw that the pigeonholes were jammed with papers, mostly correspondence. She quickly went through the letters. Some were from ranch suppliers and catalogue companies. Others were newsletters from horse and cattle breeders. Molly also found Streeter had received a number of requests for support from politicians in Helena as well as in Washington, D.C.

She closed the desk top and went through the drawers. They were filled with order forms from various mail-order companies and voluminous records of the payroll, profit and loss, and all the transactions involved in the operation of the ranch. Streeter kept meticulous records, Molly thought, seeing that no document here implicated the rancher in a murder.

No document, perhaps, but as Molly's gaze went to a side table she saw something else that did. On the table were upturned glasses, a decanter of bourbon, a cigar humidor, and a silver ashtray. In the ashtray were several cigarillo butts.

Molly picked one out of the ashtray, noting all were of the same length. A man of habit. Streeter smoked them down to a certain length, then extinguished them. The one she had found on the rocky ridge was exactly like these.

A feminine gasp took Molly's attention to the door. She saw Jane standing there, hand to her mouth. The maid must have seen the door ajar and opened it.

Molly smiled at her. She crossed the room toward the door, slipping the cigarillo butt into her skirt pocket.

"Hello, Jane," she said pleasantly.

"You shouldn't be here," Jane said, lowering her hand.

"I'm visiting the Streeters," Molly said. "Are they still upstairs?"

Jane nodded. "Something has happened. I don't know what. But the lady isn't expecting company."

"Oh, she knows I'm here," Molly said.

Jane looked at her, confused and suspicious.

Molly's eye was caught by a hunting rifle in a rack on the wall by the door. She had not seen it when she entered the office.

The polished wood stock had a distinctive swirl highlighting the grain, and the long-barreled weapon was equipped with a telescopic sight.

"That's a beautiful rifle, isn't it?" Molly said, walking to the gun rack. "I suppose you have to dust it, along with all these animal heads staring down at us."

Jane nodded, venturing a smile.

"Does Mr. Streeter use this gun often?" Molly asked. She stood on her tiptoes and read the numbers stamped into blued steel.

"I don't know," Jane said.

Molly smiled at her as she came to the door. "Well, I suppose you'd notice if the gun was not here, wouldn't you?"

"I only clean in here once a week or so," Jane said. "Really, ma'am, Mr. Streeter doesn't let hardly anyone in his office."

"Don't worry, I'm leaving," Molly said. "I won't get you in trouble." She stepped out into the hall, and Jane pulled the door shut. "You cleaned in there a week ago?"

"I don't remember," Jane said. "I've been so busy with spring cleaning."

"How about four days ago?" Molly asked. "Did you dust in there then?"

Jane thought. "No, ma'am, I don't believe I did. Mrs. Streeter and I have been going through this house from top to bottom, and I don't think I cleaned the office since two weeks ago." She asked, "Is it dirty?"

"Looked spotless to me," Molly said with a wink. She moved down the hall to the entryway. "I suppose I'll have to go now if I'm going to get back to Wolf Ridge at a decent hour. Tell Mrs. Streeter that I'm sorry I couldn't stay longer."

"Yes, ma'am," Jane said.

Molly went outside to her waiting horse. Her heart raced. The hunting rifle in Streeter's office was a .44-.40 caliber.

CHAPTER XIX

At nightfall Molly rode through Wolf Ridge on Main Street. Wood smoke was in the air, and cooking odors wafted to her, making her ravenously hungry. But supper would have to wait. She angled across Main Street and drew rein in front of the county sheriff's office.

A lamp burned inside. Through the window Molly saw the top of Sheriff Willard Jenkins' bald head as he bent over his cluttered desk. She swung down and tied the horse's reins to the rail. She stepped up onto the boardwalk, but before she could move to the door she was hailed from across the street.

Molly turned and saw Asa Lemmon come out of The Montanan. He hurried across the rutted street, pulling an envelope out of his coat pocket.

"Where the devil have you been?" he asked, thrusting the envelope at her.

"I was just getting ready to tell that to Sheriff Jenkins," Molly said. She took the envelope from his outstretched hand.

"That came by wire last night," Lemmon said. "I've been looking for you ever since."

Molly opened the sealed envelope, wondering if his position with the NA&P gave him access to all the messages that came across the wire. This one was from Horace Fenton in New York City.

Operative Molly Owens:
Received your report. Will comply with your request. Will send information from Chicago as soon as available. If you require assistance in Wolf Ridge, operatives will be dispatched posthaste.
Horace J. Fenton, Pres.
Fenton Investigative Agency
New York City, New York

Molly slid the message back into its envelope and put it in her skirt pocket. As she did so, her fingers touched the cigarillo butt from the ashtray in Sam Streeter's office.

"Mind if I listen to what you say to Jenkins?" Lemmon asked. When she hesitated, he said, "This has something to do with Pres's murder doesn't it?"

She nodded. She had agreed to work with him. "You might as well hear it firsthand."

Sheriff Jenkins looked up from his paperwork when the door opened. He greeted

Molly and cast a guarded nod at Asa Lemmon. "What can I do for you?" he said, directing the question to Molly.

"I want to bring you up to date on my investigation," she replied.

Jenkins pushed a stack of papers away and rested his elbows on the desk top. "All right. Let's hear it."

"First, I want to see the evidence I brought in from the murder scene," she said.

Jenkins nodded. Reaching down to his right, he opened a desk drawer and pulled out a large envelope with a name lettered across the top: "Preston Brooks." Inside were the brass shell casing and the cigarillo butt. He set them on the desk in front of him and looked at Molly expectantly.

Molly reached into her skirt pocket. She brought out the cigarillo butt and set it on the desk top beside the other. They were identical; even the depth of the teeth marks impressed into the dried tobacco were the same.

"Where did you find this one?" Jenkins asked.

"In an ashtray," Molly said, "in Sam Streeter's office." She pointed to the shell casing. "Streeter also owns a hunting rifle with a telescopic sight — .44-.40 caliber."

Lemmon came forward. He picked up the shell casing and examined it, then his gaze went to the cigarillo butts. Realizing the implication, he swore excitedly.

"Now, hold on," Jenkins said. "Before we go jumping to any wild conclusions, I want to hear the whole story. Just what were you doing out there at the Bar S Bar Ranch? I'm surprised Sam would even let you on the place."

Molly handed over the penciled note that had been slipped under her door night before last and described what had happened to her in the last forty-eight hours. When she finished, Sheriff Jenkins slapped a hand down on the desk top.

"I've never had much use for Welch," he said, "and this gives me the excuse I need to run him in." He shook his head. "I don't know what the hell Sam was thinking."

"I won't press charges against Buster," Molly said.

"Why not?" he asked, surprised. "You've got every right to put him away."

"That was between us," Molly said. "The score's settled."

Asa Lemmon leaned over the sheriff's desk. "I say bring him in," he said with a glance at Molly. "The prosecution will need his testimony."

186

"Prosecution?" Jenkins said. "What're you talking about?"

"I'm talking about Sam Streeter's trial," Lemmon said. "Don't you see? Miss Owens here has laid out the case right in front of you."

"I see some circumstantial evidence laid out in front of me, Mr. Lemmon," Jenkins said.

"Circumstantial, hell!" Lemmon exclaimed. "Look at those cigar butts. They're the same, a perfect match. And that rifle Miss Owens described is probably one of the few in the whole state with enough range to kill Preston Brooks from three hundred yards."

"That doesn't add up to murder," Jenkins said.

"A judge and jury will decide that," Asa Lemmon said angrily. "Listen, sheriff, I know how you feel about the ranchers around here, but you either do your sworn duty and bring Streeter in, or I'll take this case to the state attorney myself —"

Jenkins stood suddenly, glaring at Lemmon. "Mister, don't you accuse me of shirking my sworn duties," he said in a voice that was low and menacing.

Asa Lemmon did not back off or even

blink. "Then do your duty, sheriff. Do it, or face the consequences."

The arrest and jailing of Sam Streeter brought a storm of controversy that swept across the state of Montana. The controversy was focused in Wolf Ridge. Outraged ranchers came to town and besieged Sheriff Jenkins with threats and accusations of disloyalty.

Other people, however, were ready if not eager to believe Streeter was guilty of murdering Preston Brooks, guilty of trying to stifle progress in eastern Montana. More than one fistfight erupted in the saloons of Wolf Ridge as cowhands confronted townspeople, with passionate, drunken arguments on both sides.

Privately, Molly thought the case against Sam Streeter was too weak to stand, and short of a confession she expected him to be released within seventy-two hours of his arrest. But after the arrival of a state prosecutor from Helena, new developments quickly changed the course of events.

The state prosecutor's name was Claus Eberhardt, and he did not look the part. But from the moment Eberhardt stepped off the train, he began asking questions in his soft-voiced way as he quietly interviewed all the principals of the case. He caught up with Molly in the lobby of The Montanan.

A short, blond man, he was bespectacled and clean-shaven. He wore a city hat of black felt, a black suit, and a starched shirt and tie, and he seemed too meek to prosecute anyone. Clearly, the trek from Helena to Wolf Ridge was a journey into the wild frontier for him.

But in the course of the interview, Molly realized that looks were deceiving. Claus Eberhardt was not a man to be trifled with. His soft-spoken questions, carrying the slightest trace of a German accent, drove to the heart of matters. He politely pried every bit of information out of her and relentlessly cross-questioned her to find out for himself how well her testimony would stand up in court.

Molly was subpoenaed soon afterward to appear at the preliminary hearing to be held in the Wolf Ridge Community Hall. Three days later, in the case of *The People of Montana* vs. *Samuel Doris Streeter*, she found out that Eberhardt could handle himself inside the courtroom as well as outside.

Streeter was represented by Alfred Wolcott, the gray-bearded mayor of Wolf

Ridge, who was an attorney by profession. He was evidently saving his fight for the trial. Aside from raising occasional objections, he sat at the table in the front of the hall beside his square-shouldered client and said little. Surprised by his silence, Molly began to suspect that the evidence about to be presented was persuasive.

She soon found out that it was. The makeshift courtroom was jammed with townspeople and ranchers. Most sat on wooden folding chairs that were used for the lively productions staged here, and others stood at the back of the hall. Still more people stood outside peering in through windows.

In the front row across the aisle from Molly, Helene Streeter sat behind her husband. Seated in the chair beside her was Judith Wolcott. She held Helene's hand. Molly recognized other women from the Decency League, and as she glanced around she noted that all walks of life were represented here, with the possible exception of the women from Lillie's place. In a corner of the room she saw Asa Lemmon.

Directly in front of Molly was the prosecutor's table, where Claus Eberhardt sat alone. On the stage ahead of the two attorneys' tables was the judge's bench, a table with a gavel on it.

Everyone in the room had stood when Judge Henry Garret entered, and they now listened with quiet intensity as he directed the proceedings. First, the court clerk read a long deposition that the prosecutor had taken from Buster Welch. The Bar S Bar foreman had been granted immunity, Eberhardt explained, and would be available for testimony during the trial.

Next Molly was called to the stand, a chair beside the judge's bench, and testified for more than an hour, recounting the details of her investigation. She was followed by several people who had witnessed the murder. They described what they had seen that day.

Eberhardt himself then discussed the physical evidence, showing the matching cigarillo butts and the shell casing. The first surprise of the day came when he launched into a discussion of the "scientific methods" he had used during his investigation. This involved a test firing of the suspected murder weapon.

The firing pin of Streeter's high-powered rifle, it turned out, was slightly misaligned, causing it to leave a unique imprint on the cap end of the shell casing. Eberhardt had established this fact with a magnifying lens, but even with the naked eye the marks on the two shell casings could be clearly seen to be the same. Eberhardt compared these two to others from the same kind of hunting rifle. They were noticeably different.

After the noon meal, Molly returned with the hordes of people to the community hall and listened to Jane testify in a shaky voice that now she did indeed remember that the hunting rifle had not been in its rack on the day of Preston Brooks' murder. Evidently Eberhardt had managed to refresh her memory on that score. Molly was chagrined that the prosecutor had uncovered important testimony that she had missed, but knew that this sort of thing was not uncommon. A witness' first reaction to a question is not always complete, and after thinking about a particular incident a witness will often recall it more clearly.

The final testimony of the day was the most surprising. And it was the most damaging. It came from one of the prospective farmers who had ridden the train out to right-of-way land the day of the murder.

This man, a lifelong farmer with iron-gray hair and a weathered face, took the stand and sat there perfectly still, holding his battered straw hat on his lap. It soon became clear why neither Sheriff Jenkins nor Molly had questioned him during their investigations. His name was Ernst Kellerman, and he spoke only German.

The day of the murder Ernst Kellerman had wandered away from the crowd. He understood nothing of the sales pitch and decided to inspect the land himself. Seeing a ravine far behind the speaker, he wondered if it held water. First he walked parallel to the railroad tracks for several hundred yards, then cut across the right-of-way, heading for the ravine.

Finding it dry, he walked over a rise just as the fatal shot was fired. Out of sight and earshot of the crowd gathered by the train, this German farmer did not realize what had happened. And from his angle he never saw a rifleman. But several minutes later movement far in the distance caught his eye. A horsebacker came out of a deep ravine.

The rider was too far away to describe with any certainty, but the horse was memorable. The animal was a cream-colored Arabian. Ernst Kellerman was absolutely certain of that because he had recently seen Arabian horses performing in a traveling circus and had been much impressed with them.

This testimony was translated for the court clerk by Claus Eberhardt and raised a hubbub in the room. Judge Garret gaveled for silence. He asked a few follow-up questions that were translated by the prosecutor, then banged the gavel once more and retired to a back dressing room that was used for judge's chambers.

Molly saw Sam Streeter conferring with Wolcott. Behind him Helene sat with her head bowed, shoulders quivering now as she wept. Murmurs from the people in the room grew louder and louder.

Molly's emotions were jumbled, and her thoughts raced. She had to admire the case Eberhardt had put together. In a sense she had been outclassed by him, even though she knew he could not have worked so quickly and efficiently without the ground-work she had completed and turned over to him.

Still, she could not help but recall Sam Streeter's fear that a murder charge would be pinned on him by a "high-priced lawyer from the NA&P." Eberhardt did not represent the railroad, but he was certainly skilled. He had built his case like a master cabinet-maker might construct a box. It was wonderfully straightforward and appeared to be airtight.

Judge Garret must have agreed. When he returned from chambers he ordered the defendant bound over for trial.

CHAPTER XX

Molly was swept out of the makeshift court-room by a crowd eager for fresh air and a chance to spread the news. In the confusion outside she found herself near Helene Streeter. The ranchwoman, her face swollen and reddened by tears, was steadied by Judith Wolcott.

Helene must have sensed Molly's presence for she turned and glared at her. Without exchanging a word the two women stopped and faced one another while the chattering crowd passed by. Helene motioned for the mayor's wife to go on.

"I befriended you, Molly," Helene said when they were alone, "and because I trusted you my husband is on trial for his life."

"Helene, that isn't true," Molly said. "I did not betray our friendship."

Helene's small mouth twisted in anger, and suddenly her hand lashed out.

Instinctively Molly raised her arm. She expertly blocked the slap aimed at her face. Helene's eyes flashed as she glowered at Molly. They stared at one another for a long moment until Helene turned abruptly and hurriedly walked away.

"A former friend makes the worst enemy."

Molly turned around and saw that Asa Lemmon had spoken. He came toward her, grinning. Molly again had the sensation that she was looking into the face of a weasel.

"You did the right thing," he went on, "testifying in there this morning. You told the truth, and that Streeter woman's going to have to swallow it."

The cavalier remark brought a wave of anger to Molly. Lemmon was clearly gloating over what he regarded to be a victory. "An arrangement of facts doesn't always add up to the whole truth," she said.

"What'd you mean by that?" he asked. "Sam Streeter's guilty of murdering Pres. Everybody knows it, and by god he'll hang for it."

"He may," Molly said, "but before that happens I'm going to ask some questions."

"What for?" he asked, smirking. "This thing's all wrapped up."

Molly walked away without replying. Something about that man left her feeling dirty. She returned to the center of town and followed the boardwalk along Main

197

Street to the county sheriff's office. She had caught a glimpse of Jenkins leading his handcuffed prisoner out a side door of the community hall and guessed they had come back here.

Alfred Wolcott came out of the lawman's office as Molly approached. She watched him cross the street, heading for a cafe. She went to the door and opened it.

Inside the office Molly was met by a stern-faced Sheriff Jenkins. He eyed her as she closed the door.

"I want to talk to Sam Streeter," she said.

Jenkins stared in surprise as though he could not believe what he had just heard. "Lady, I can tell you for a certain fact that you're just about the last person on this earth Sam wants to see."

"Tell him I'm here as a friend," she said, realizing as she spoke that her words sounded ludicrous.

Jenkins shook his head. "Sam's been through enough today without this."

"Then will you give him the message?" Molly asked. "It's important that I talk to him."

"All right," Jenkins said, exhaling loudly, "I'll tell him. But not now. He's trying to get some shuteye." Jerking his bald head toward the hotel across the street, Jenkins said, "I reckon I know where to find you."

From the county sheriff's office Molly went to the NA&P depot and telegraphed a message to New York. She brought Horace Fenton up to date on the day's legal proceedings and without explanation informed him that she planned to remain in Wolf Ridge for a few more days.

Back at The Montanan Molly ate supper in the dining room and then went up to her room. She lay on the bed as the room darkened, trying to sort things out. Her thoughts were interrupted by a rap on the door.

"Who is it?" she asked, sitting up.

"Jenkins, Sheriff Jenkins."

Molly left the bed and went to the door. She found Jenkins standing in the hall, hat pushed back on his forehead, thumbs hooked through his gunbelt.

"Sam says he'll talk to you," he said. "Lord knows why."

Molly left the hotel with Jenkins. They crossed the darkened main street and went into his office. The cellblock was in the rear of the building. Jenkins unlocked an ironclad door at the back of the room and motioned for Molly to enter.

She stepped inside, hearing a man snoring. The dimly lit room reeked of vomit and unwashed men. Her eyes slowly adjusted to the faint light and she saw half a dozen steel-barred cells in a row. In the nearest one a squat figure sat on the bunk, his big shoulders hunched as though cold.

"Here she is, Sam," Jenkins said, stopping in front of that cell. "Soon as you want her to leave, give me a holler." The lawman's tone of voice was warm, that of one longtime friend to another.

Molly watched the squat figure rise up out of the gloom and come to the barred door of the cell. She approached the bars while Jenkins backed away. The sheriff left the cellblock but did not close the reinforced door.

Sam Streeter regarded Molly. He still wore his suit from the day in the courtroom, but he had removed his tie. For several moments the only sound in the cellblock was the dry, rhythmic snoring of a prisoner in another cage.

Molly said, "You didn't kill Preston Brooks, did you?"

Streeter grasped the bars and gave the cell door a violent, futile shake. "You and that little prosecutor nailed my coffin shut today, and now you come in here and tell the truth. What the hell is your game?"

"No game," Molly said. "I gave the facts of my investigation when I testified. Now I want to continue my investigation. You can help me."

"How?" Streeter demanded.

"By telling me everything you know," Molly said. "And I mean everything. Hold nothing back."

Streeter glared at her, his distrust obvious. "My lawyer told me not to say anything until the trial. That's why I had to sit there all day without saying a damned word in my own defense."

"Maybe you should take your attorney's advice," Molly said.

"Maybe I should," Streeter said, not taking his eyes from her. "But what do you have in mind?"

"Just what I told you," Molly said. "I want to go on with my investigation into the murder of Preston Brooks." She paused. "I don't have much to go on. I want you to understand that I didn't come here to make any promises. I'm looking for information."

Streeter nodded curtly. "You do have your ways of getting information, don't you? You lied to me, and you took advantage of my wife. And because of you, one of my line shacks was burned to the ground."

"I'm not the one who invited those outlaws to stay there," Molly said.

"Outlaws," Streeter repeated.

"You knew those men were a step ahead of the law, didn't you?" Molly asked. "And if they robbed NA&P trains, so much the better."

"Don't you accuse me —"

"I'm not accusing you of anything," Molly interrupted. "I'm saying we'd better be honest with one another."

"A lot you know about honesty," Streeter said. "You're a sneak and a liar. And now you come along and tell me you're on my side."

"I'm not on anyone's side," Molly said. "I'm trying to get at the truth, that's all."

Streeter paused, considering that. "What's in it for you — a reward from the North American and Pacific?"

Molly shook her head.

"Then who's paying you?" he demanded.

"That isn't important," Molly said. "Let's just say I won't rest easy until Preston Brooks' murderer is brought to justice."

Streeter grunted, stepping back from the cell door. In a gesture of frustration he slapped his hands together.

Molly understood his dilemma. His defense had been laid out for him by Alfred Wolcott, and he was prepared for a trial. But now he saw a glimmer of hope, one that his attorney would almost certainly not approve. Streeter's loyalties were clashing as he eyed Molly, weighing his distrust of her against his enormous desire to get out of this stinking cage.

Slapping his chunky hands together again, he came toward her like a bull charging a corral fence. He grasped the bars and uttered a curse. "Can't see that I've got much to lose now. What do you want to know?"

CHAPTER XXI

Molly left the county sheriff's office after spending nearly an hour with Sam Streeter. She crossed Main Street, breathing deeply of the cool and clean night air, convinced now that the ranchman stood falsely accused. The facts to prove his innocence, however, were slim.

The Arabian Streeter used as a saddle horse was lame the day of Preston Brooks' murder, and he'd left the animal in a stall in the horse barn. After saddling another horse, a black gelding, he'd picked up the lunch Helene had packed and ridden alone to the west sector of the ranch.

Streeter spent the day searching for a prize bull he believed had strayed in that direction. He rode all day without seeing another soul and did not return to the home ranch until late in the evening. He came back empty-handed. And he had not taken his hunting rifle with him.

Under the right circumstances anyone could be driven by rage or revenge to kill, Molly supposed, but the murder of Preston Brooks had been a deliberate, calculated act. Streeter might be capable of doing such a thing, but he would certainly have been smart enough to have arranged a solid alibi. He would not have relied on a simple denial.

At this point a denial was about all Sam Streeter had to take into court. Evidently his attorney hoped to raise a reasonable doubt in the minds of jurors and rely on character witnesses and local sympathy to save his client from the hangman.

At best, Molly thought, as she entered the lobby of The Montanan, that was a risky defense. Claus Eberhardt was a very persuasive man, and as a skillful prosecutor representing "the people of Montana," he would undoubtedly portray Streeter as a coldhearted murderer, a man undeserving of sympathy.

Molly climbed the stairs to her room. She undressed, blew out the lamp, and got into bed. Her thoughts were racing, but she was too tired to stay awake. As she fell asleep, she realized she was beginning to think about the case in a new way, one that pulled her investigation in a different direction.

Someone had devised a plan to make Sam Streeter look guilty of murder. Who?

Early in the morning Molly rented a

saddle horse from the livery and made a hard ride for the Bar S Bar Ranch.

As she came over the rise overlooking the ranch headquarters, she saw that from outward appearances nothing had changed. Corrals and fenced pastures held muscular, deep-chested bulls, as well as Percheron and Arabian horses. All was neat and orderly, from the painted buildings to the stacks of logs and firewood. The great stone house stood in the shade of tall cottonwood trees like a monument.

Molly rode to the house and dismounted. She went to the front door and knocked. When no response came to her second knock, she walked around the big house, stepping over freshly turned flower beds by the picket fence, and rapped loudly on the back door. Repeated knocks brought no answer.

Molly turned and looked at the outbuildings. The big sliding door of the barn stood open. She caught a glimpse of movement in the runway there and sensed that someone had been watching her.

Whoever it was had ducked back into the darkness of the barn. Molly drew her .38 from the shoulder holster under her jacket and walked down there.

She moved to the side of the doorway

and eased around the doorjamb, revolver held at the ready. In the pungent shadows she saw horse stalls and a tack room where gear was stored and repaired.

"Come out," Molly said loudly. For a long moment nothing happened. She heard a horse stamp his hoof. But then someone slowly came out of the shadows. He stepped into the runway and walked toward the wide door. As he drew near, Molly recognized him. It was Buster Welch.

"What're you doing here, Buster?" she asked, lowering the revolver.

"I run this outfit," he replied with a trace of indignation.

"Last time I saw you," Molly said, "you were ready to pack your war bag and ride."

"Turned out I was needed around here," he said. "I'm the only man on the place who can run things until . . . until the trial's over."

"I see," Molly said. "You came out of this thing smelling like a rose, didn't you, Buster?"

Welch gave her a blank stare in reply, his gaze moving down the length of her body. "You can holster that gun. I ain't gonna hurt you none."

"I know you aren't, Buster," Molly said.

She made no move to return the .38 to her shoulder holster. "Up at the house I knocked on the door, but I couldn't raise anyone."

"Mrs. Streeter, she's staying with the Wolcotts in town," he said.

"The maid must be around here," Molly said.

Welch shook his head. "Mrs. Streeter fired that girl. I hear the prosecutor's keeping her in town somewhere. What do you want to talk to her for?"

"I have a few questions I'd like to ask her," Molly said. "Just like I have a few for you."

"Me?" he said defensively. "Sheriff Jenkins already cleared me. I was out on the range with the hands the day Brooks got it."

"All day?" Molly asked.

"Yeah," he said, "the whole damned day. Got witnesses to prove it."

"That was the day Sam Streeter was hunting for a bull," Molly said.

"I know," Welch said.

"Was the animal ever found?" Molly asked.

"Oh, sure," Welch replied. "Some of the hands came across that critter in a gulch — dead."

"What did it die of?" she asked.

"Some yokel shot him," he said with a shrug. "It happens. Somebody riding through Bar S Bar range, maybe doesn't like Streeter or ranchers in general, and takes a shot at some stock. Lost a couple of good horses that way last year — Percherons. You should have seen Streeter. Talk about mad." Welch added with a cocky air, "That's why he needs me around here. I can take care of things and manage men."

"I'm sure you're doing a wonderful job, Buster," Molly said.

The foreman regarded her with suspicion.

"You think your boss is guilty?" she asked.

Welch shrugged again.

"You don't seem too upset about his arrest," Molly said.

"You know how Streeter is," he said. "The man has a powerful temper. When things don't go the way he figures they ought to, there's hell to pay." He added, "Hell, I don't know if he's guilty. All I know is, he had reason. He could have done it. That don't mean I want him to hang."

Welch moved past her. "Now, if you don't mind, I've got work to do, a whole pile of it. And I've got a temperamental mess cook to contend with. I wish Miz Streeter was here. She could always handle him, don't think she couldn't."

Molly watched the foreman walk away, heading for the mess hall. She holstered her revolver.

Molly rode back to Wolf Ridge, arriving at the livery stable late in the afternoon. She returned to The Montanan and took a hot bath. Refreshed and wearing a navy-blue dress of serge with lace trim, she went downstairs to the dining room. After ordering a glass of red wine, she decided on a steak with a baked potato and tossed salad for supper.

Molly raised the glass to her lips. The first taste of the French wine was on her tongue when a woman came to the table. Molly looked up and saw Helene Streeter. She lowered the glass.

"I spoke to Sam this morning," Helene said in a subdued voice, "and I've been looking for you all day." She bit her lip. "I owe you an apology, Molly. I shouldn't have said those things yesterday . . ."

Molly raised the wine glass to her. "Let's put it in the past, Helene. Will you join me for supper?"

"Thank you, I believe I will," she replied. She pulled out the chair across from Molly

210

and sat down. "I haven't had a full meal since the day Sam was arrested. Judith thinks I'm wasting away. Food just doesn't seem important."

"That's understandable," Molly said.

Helene leaned forward on her elbows. "Sam told me you're still investigating the murder. You don't think he's guilty, do you?"

"No, I don't," Molly said, signaling the waitress to bring another glass of wine.

"Who do you suspect?" Helene asked.

"I'm not ready to name anyone," Molly said. "I'm still asking questions."

"But you must believe someone around here is a murderer," Helene said. "Someone on our ranch, or is it someone here in town?"

"I wish I knew," Molly said.

Helene looked dejected as a glass of red wine was placed on the table in front of her. "I was hoping you were hot on a trail. Molly, I'm scared to death of what will happen if Sam goes to trial." She snatched up the glass and drained half the wine.

"I went out to the ranch today," Molly said.

Helene's eyes widened over the glass, and she abruptly set it down. "Whatever for?"

"I wanted to talk to Jane," Molly said.

"Why, may I ask?" she said.

"I got to wondering if she knew more than what came out in the hearing yesterday," Molly said, "and wanted to question her. Apparently Claus Eberhardt has put her away somewhere for safekeeping."

"I fired that ungrateful girl," Helene said, "and ordered her off our property for her disloyalty." She added indignantly, "And after all I did for her."

Molly watched as Helene finished the wine in her glass. The alcohol brought a flush to her cheeks.

"I'd like to hear her account for her actions on the day of the murder," Molly said.

"I can account for them," Helene said.

"What do you mean?" Molly asked. "You were with her all day?"

"I certainly wasn't," Helene said. "That was her day off. Once a month Jane goes to town for a day, and that was her day. Some nerve, she has, saying that she remembers Sam's rifle was gone. Jane didn't come back until late in the evening. Don't you think she was just a bit too eager to tell all? She was trying to embarrass us, don't you think? Ungrateful wretch."

Helene looked around for the waitress. "I'm hungry. Suddenly I feel absolutely famished."

CHAPTER XXII

Helene Streeter's anger toward her maid was not surprising, Molly thought, as they parted in the lobby of The Montanan. Helene was a proud woman, and much of her privacy, her decorum, had been stripped bare in the courtroom when Jane had testified so freely about the routine in the Streeter household as well as the disappearance of the hunting rifle.

Helene's blind allegiance to her husband, though, did surprise Molly a little. She well remembered the air of tension in the stately ranch house, and Helene's abrupt change of mood when her husband was present.

But perhaps she should not find that loyalty so surprising, Molly thought, as she turned and started across the hotel lobby to the staircase. As a Fenton operative, she had been involved in a number of domestic disputes and had witnessed this phenomenon before. A wife could be at her husband's throat until he was arrested, and suddenly she would become his staunchest defender.

Deep in her thoughts, Molly did not notice the figure crossing the lobby on a course to intercept her. At the bottom of the staircase a man blocked her path.

"Evening," Asa Lemmon said.

Molly was briefly startled, instantly realizing that he must have been watching her for some time. "Are you following me or Helene Streeter?"

His small dark eyes narrowing to slits, he asked, "Just what do you mean by that?"

"The last two times I've been with Helene," Molly said, "you've appeared out of nowhere. Quite a coincidence."

"Now, hold on," he said. "You've got the wrong notion. I was sitting here in the lobby waiting for you. We need to talk — alone."

"What about?" she asked.

He studied her. "No reason to be unfriendly. I want to know how your investigation is going. Turned up any new suspects?"

"I have some ideas," Molly said.

"Well, what are they?" Lemmon asked. "Look, we're on the same side. We both want Pres's killer to stretch a rope, don't we?"

"I thought you were satisfied that the guilty man was under indictment," Molly said.

"Sure, I am," Lemmon said. "But I know you believe otherwise. As chief of western operations for the NA&P, I figure I've got a right to know what you're doing."

Molly was ready to argue that point, but as she looked at him she heard the distant wail of a train whistle. The sound stirred her, coming again like a mournful cry.

Molly's pulse quickened. Somehow the mournful sound of the train whistle brought a new theory to her mind, one that might answer a lot of questions.

"The truth is," she said, "I do have a suspect."

"Who?" Lemmon asked.

"For now I'll have to keep the suspect's identity to myself," Molly said.

Lemmon moved closer to her. "We'll keep this between us. Who is it?"

Molly shook her head. "I need to do some more groundwork. No sense in taking a chance that someone will be falsely accused."

"Look, I want to know," he said. "Maybe I can help out. You need a man's help in this case, don't you?"

"So far I've managed without it," Molly said. She added, "If I need help, you'll be the first to know."

Lemmon's jaw tightened. The train

whistle sounded again, louder now. He was reluctant to leave without an answer, but after glowering at her for a long moment, he turned away and mounted the stairs.

Molly watched Lemmon turn at the landing and head toward his suite. Her heart pounded. He had been very persistent in questioning her. That had struck an odd note. For some reason she had made a connection at the sound of the steam engine's whistle.

A ghostly call from Preston Brooks, she thought. The idea ran a chill up her spine. As she had looked into Lemmon's eyes she suddenly realized he was a man who possessed the dark qualities of a cold-blooded killer, an assassin.

The day the outlaws were flushed from the burning cabin she had seen Asa Lemmon kill without hesitation or remorse. And she had often sensed he was a man of great cunning. Now she believed that he was the one man here capable of devising the complicated scheme that made Sam Streeter appear guilty of murder.

But she was going on instinct. She tried to think it through, testing the theory against what she knew. As she considered what had to be done to make Streeter look guilty of murder, from the shooting of the bull to the theft of his rifle and Arabian horse, she realized Lemmon couldn't have done it alone. He might have devised the plan, but he couldn't have executed it by himself. Not all of it.

Who helped him? When Molly thought about what had to be done to make the plan work, one name came to her mind: Buster Welch.

The pieces of the puzzle did fit together. Welch disliked his boss, and Molly had been struck by his indifference toward Streeter's arrest. She supposed Lemmon had come to the foreman with a foolproof plan and some sort of incentive — money or land — and all Welch had to do was set the thing in motion.

First he'd herded the bull to a remote gulch and shot it. He'd made it appear that the animal had wandered off to the west sector of the ranch, knowing full well that Streeter would ride hell for leather after it. All that was left was to make off with his boss's hunting rifle and saddle horse. That wasn't difficult because the maid wasn't in the house, and the only person he had to get past was Helene Streeter. If she was outside working on her flowers, that would be a simple task.

Welch rode out, leading the Arabian, and met Lemmon at a prearranged spot. Welch would then return to the cowhands he supervised, keeping his alibi intact.

Lemmon had murdered Preston Brooks, and had been in no hurry to leave the scene. He couldn't be, riding a lame horse. What a stroke of luck, to be seen from a distance by the German farmer. Or perhaps Lemmon had seen the man first, and had set up the sighting.

It was well planned, Molly thought, even to the fine point of leaving one of Streeter's cigarillo butts behind. Probably Lemmon expected Sheriff Jenkins to find it; he must have had a bad moment when Jenkins couldn't even pick up the trail. Molly had unwittingly helped out there. She had not only found the trail, but had come to the conclusion Lemmon wanted when he had ridden back to the Bar S Bar, where he must have turned the horse and rifle over to Buster Welch. Lemmon had then returned to town on his own mount while Welch had sneaked the Arabian back into his stall and the hunting rifle onto the rack in Streeter's office.

The theory certainly explained Lemmon's intense interest in Molly's investigation. His scheme was running like clockwork, and now she was threatening to throw a monkey wrench into the works.

As sound as this theory was, Molly thought, it raised one unanswered question — motive. What did Asa Lemmon have to gain by the death of Preston Brooks?

Certainly Lemmon's position with the North American & Pacific Railroad had improved since the murder. He was no longer a clerk working as an assistant to Brooks. Now, as he had been quick to point out, he was chief of western operations for the company. But could Lemmon have known he would receive that appointment in the event of Brooks' death?

Molly needed help to answer that question. She left the hotel and went to the telegraph office in the train depot. On the way she smelled night air that was fragrant with the odor of coal smoke from the steam engine. A long line of freight cars stood on the tracks beyond the depot.

Hearing the hissing locomotive there, Molly vividly recalled that she had often met Pres at night amid the sounds and smells of his private train. The memory was etched so clearly in her mind that she again felt a strange, ghostly presence.

At the telegrapher's window inside the depot Molly wrote her message and watched the telegrapher tap it out with his key. Besides a brief report to Horace Fenton, she asked for a complete background check on Asa Lemmon and his status with the NA&P.

Late that night Molly slipped into a troubled, tossing sleep. Before dawn she came awake and sat up in bed. She knew that if she could somehow link Asa Lemmon and Buster Welch, that would be important evidence to back up her theory. She wondered if some sort of written agreement existed between the two men.

Unable to sleep, she decided to find out. She dressed in the dark and left The Montanan by a back staircase, a fire exit that opened into the alley. The night was silent and very dark. Overhead stars were pinpoints of white light in a black sky.

By the light of those stars Molly saw that the alley was clear. She stepped out from the night shadow cast by the hotel and followed the narrow alley to the rear entrance of the homestead locator office. She reached for the door handle and then touched the keyhole under it with her fingertips.

Molly pulled a ring of master skeleton keys out of her handbag. Working blindly, she began trying them in the door. The sixth one slid easily into the keyhole. Turning the key, she heard the lock release with a *click*, surprisingly loud.

Molly glanced up and down the alley. Night silence had magnified the sound. In the starlit shadows she saw no movement and heard nothing. She turned the door handle. Tiptoeing inside, she eased the door closed.

Molly stood in the complete darkness of what she guessed to be a back room, listening. Lemmon's assistant might bunk here, she thought, and for several minutes she listened intently for the sounds of a sleeping man.

Hearing nothing, Molly moved slowly ahead, feeling her way through the darkness like a blind woman. Her outstretched hands touched a plank wall.

Molly slid her fingers along the unpapered wall until she felt the vertical framing of a doorjamb. She reached down for the handle, found it, and slowly opened the door, listening intently.

In the silence of this darkened office faint starlight filtered in through the front windows. She saw the dim shapes of the map table, chairs, and several filing cabinets. On the table she saw the glint of glass. A lamp was there.

Molly fumbled through her handbag until she found matches. She drew one out as she moved to the map table. Lifting the glass chimney off the lamp, she struck the match and touched the flaring flame to the wick.

The light was too bright, and she immediately turned the wick down as far as possible without extinguishing the flame. Now Molly saw her own reflection in the windows. She knew that lamplight spilled out onto the boardwalk and the street.

She took a deep breath and hurried to the filing cabinets. She would have to work fast and trust to luck that the night deputy had already made his rounds.

Molly soon discovered that none of the filing cabinets were locked, and that worked in her favor. But as she held the lamp in one hand and flipped through the records, she gradually realized that no incriminating evidence was likely to be here.

She looked around the room. No floor safe was in this place, not even a desk with locked drawers. The office was strictly for processing the sale of right-of-way land. She carried the lamp into the back room, where she had first entered. She held it high and looked around. Rolled maps lay in a far corner. Otherwise the room was empty.

The hollow sounds of boots on the boardwalk made her lower the lamp and quickly blow out the flame. Someone had come from the street onto the boardwalk, and now the front door rattled.

Molly stood still. She saw a man press his face against the glass as he tried to see inside. He carried a stubby weapon that she recognized as a sawed-off shotgun. When he stepped back, Molly saw the glint of a badge on his vest.

The night deputy moved swiftly away from the window to the side of the building. Molly knew he was headed for the back door. And she knew that he would find it unlocked.

CHAPTER XXIII

Molly set the lamp down on the floor and stepped into the office, closing the door to the back room behind her. Dodging around the big map table, she rushed through the office to the front door. As she felt for the lock release under the door knob, she heard the back door bang open.

"Come out!" the night deputy ordered. "Come out, or I'll shoot!"

Molly's fingers fumbled over the door lock in the ensuing silence. The scrape of a boot heel on the floor told her that the deputy had entered the back room. A moment later she heard the crash of glass followed by a muttered curse. The deputy had kicked over the lamp she had left behind.

Molly turned the lock one way and then the other, and the door opened. She ran outside, pounding across the boardwalk to the street. Handbag flapping against her side, she sprinted down the street toward The Montanan. Between the darkened hotel and a store next door was a passageway several feet wide. She dashed in there and ran for the alley.

Behind her, Molly heard the deputy curse and knew from his exasperated tone that he had not seen which way she had gone. At the alley she turned toward the hotel and ran past fire barrels filled with water to the rear entrance of The Montanan.

Molly took the stairs two at a time. Entering the second-floor hallway, she hurried to her room, pulling her key out of her handbag. She unlocked the door and went in. She closed the door and leaned against it, breathing hard.

She had not found one shred of incriminating evidence against Asa Lemmon, but perhaps she had accomplished something else by playing that dangerous game with the night deputy. In the morning Lemmon would be notified of the break-in. If he was innocent, he would regard it as nothing more than an attempted burglary.

But if he was hiding a crime, a murder, now he would conclude that someone was on his trail. He might suspect Molly, but would not know for certain who had searched his office. Molly hoped that doubt would prey on his mind. It might make him do something foolish, something that would point to his guilt.

Early in the morning, Saturday, Molly opened her door a crack. While she kept a watch, several hotel guests left their rooms and went downstairs for breakfast. Presently she heard voices at the far end of the hall, toward Lemmon's suite. She put her ear to the crack and recognized the voice of Sheriff Jenkins. The lawman was at the door of the suite.

When the two men left the hotel, Molly picked up her handbag and looked out into the hall. Seeing that it was clear, she quickly moved to Lemmon's door. She reached into her handbag and found the set of lock probes.

She judged that Lemmon would be gone for several minutes while inspecting the homestead locator office with Sheriff Jenkins, and that would be enough time for a quick search of his belongings. All she had to do was get through the hotel lock.

The door locks in The Montanan were modern, not the skeleton-key type she had encountered last night. Molly had already experimented with the lock in her door, and had the probe that had worked in hand when she reached the door of Lemmon's suite.

Like a dentist's tool, the tip of fine steel curved to a point. Molly inserted it into the lock. Just then the door to her right opened.

Molly quickly straightened up and casually knocked on Lemmon's door. A young couple came out of the adjacent room, briefly surprised to see someone in the hall. Molly cast a smile at them, then faced the door as though expecting someone to answer.

The young man and woman, honeymooners perhaps, were more interested in one another than in a stranger in the hall, and after closing the door to their room they walked away and descended the staircase.

Molly bent down. She probed the lock with the steel instrument, drawing it out as she exerted upward pressure. The mechanism released. Turning the lock, she grasped the door handle and turned it. The door opened.

Molly withdrew the probe and quickly stepped inside, closing the door behind her. Much more spacious than her room, this suite was similarly decorated and furnished with a brass bed, a walnut dresser, a matching wash stand, and a large closet.

Molly searched the closet first, then went through the dresser drawers. She found nothing but clothes, shoes and boots, and a box of .32-caliber ammunition. Lemmon evidently carried a small handgun.

No papers were here, certainly nothing incriminating that would link Lemmon and Buster Welch in a conspiracy to murder the railroad tycoon.

Molly started for the door and then turned back to survey the room. Except for the unmade bed, all was neat and orderly, just as she found the room. Now she thought that if she was going to put pressure on Lemmon she would have to let him discover the fact that his room had been searched.

She went to the dresser and pulled two of the drawers out several inches. In the closet she took a pair of trousers off a hanger and let them fall to the floor. Then she left the suite, locking the door behind her.

After breakfast Molly kept a discreet watch on the homestead locator office. She had seen Lemmon and his clerk go inside, and through the morning several men dressed in overalls and straw hats went in there.

Saturday shoppers from outlying farms and ranches filled the boardwalks, and their wagons and horses jammed Main Street. The people were here to buy a week's supply of necessities and the few luxuries they could afford. Wagons were parked all around the false-fronted stores, and down by the depot Geary's Hardware & Ranch Supply looked like a human beehive, with people constantly going in and out.

Cowhands came to town in the afternoon, freshly shaved and shorn. They sported their best shirts and clean Levi's. Molly watched the weathered young men pick their way through the traffic on Main Street as they rode toward the saloon district. They were a breed all their own, she thought, as spirited as their cow ponies, and they had come to town for a good time.

In the middle of the afternoon Molly saw two big freight wagons from the Bar S Bar roll into town. They were led by Buster Welch. One wagon went on to Geary's, and the other pulled up at a general store. Welch reined up in front of the county sheriff's office.

Molly watched the foreman go inside, guessing that he would report to Sam Streeter. Molly moved into the doorway of a dress shop where she could keep an eye on both the homestead locator office and the door of Jenkins' office.

Twenty minutes later Buster Welch came out. He made his way out to the edge of the boardwalk, elbowing past a pair of farmers, and stood there as he surveyed the street. Molly turned away and peered into the window, where a long dress was mounted on a mannequin. Out of the corner of her eye she saw Welch cross Main Street after a freight wagon passed by.

She turned around and saw him head for a side street that led to the saloon district. Disappointed, she left the doorway and moved along the boardwalk far enough to see him cut across that street at an angle. He entered a gambling parlor called Devil's Luck. She had hoped that Welch would try to make contact with Lemmon, verifying her theory.

No such luck. Buster Welch remained in the saloon district until nightfall, and Asa Lemmon worked late with his clerk, dined in The Montanan, and went up to his suite with a bottle tucked under his arm.

Molly went into her own room, wondering what was running through the man's mind now that he'd had time to discover the fact that someone had gone through his belongings. Three-quarters of an hour later a knock came at her door. She opened it, expecting to find an angry Asa Lemmon there. Instead Helene

Streeter stood in the hall.

"I hope you don't mind my coming by on the spur of the moment," she said.

"Not at all, Helene," Molly said. "Come in."

Helene Streeter entered the room somewhat tentatively as she glanced about. "Very nice," she murmured. "I've never actually been inside one of these rooms, you know." She added with a slight smile, "Sam's law."

"How is he?" Molly asked, showing her to the one chair in the room.

"Not well," Helene replied, sitting down. "Sam is a man who hates being cooped up. Even in the ranch house on a wintry day he would get into a dark mood. Now . . ." Her voice trailed off. "That's why I'm here, Molly, to find out if you can offer any hope, any little tidbit that might raise his spirits."

"I'm afraid I can't, Helene," Molly said. "I don't know any more now than I did yesterday."

"But surely you must know something," Helene said. "Otherwise you wouldn't be so certain my Sam is innocent."

"I don't have any evidence that points to a killer — yet," Molly said.

"Well, at least tell me what you're thinking," Helene said. She smiled. "We're friends, aren't we? After all, if you can't confide in your friends, what good are they?"

"I have some theories," Molly said, "but I can't discuss them."

"Please, Molly," she said, leaning forward in the chair, "I beg you. Tell me about these theories of yours."

She was on the edge of tears, and Molly reached out and held her trembling hand. "Helene, I'm working on this case day and night, and I assure you that when I uncover solid evidence that points to the killer, I'll tell you as soon as I can."

As Helene nodded in reply, Molly heard a soft scraping sound on the door. Touching a finger to her lips, Molly turned around and picked up her handbag on the bed. She drew out her .38 and moved silently to the door. Grasping the handle, she slowly turned it. She yanked the door open.

Crouched in the hall was Asa Lemmon. With a look of surprise on his face, he nearly fell into the room.

"What's going on?" Helene shrieked, leaving the chair. "What do you want?"

"He wanted to hear what we were saying," Molly said as Asa Lemmon straightened up. "Isn't that right, Mr. Lemmon?"

"I heard voices in here," he said, obviously searching for words, "and thought you might need assistance."

"You were snooping!" Helene exclaimed. "Spying on us!"

"That was not my intention, Mrs. Streeter," he said, backing away, "but I can see you're too upset to hear me out —"

"I'll hear you out," Helene interrupted. "Just what do you have to say for yourself?"

He stopped. "I have been concerned that Molly — Miss Owens — is in some danger because of her investigation, and just now when I passed by her door and heard voices —"

"I don't believe a word you're saying!" Helene said. She whirled to Molly. "Do you?"

Before Molly could reply, Lemmon backed out of the doorway. He turned and strode away, heading for his suite.

"The nerve of that man!" Helene exclaimed.

Molly closed the door. Seeing Helene's distraught expression, she wished she could now explain why Asa Lemmon was her chief suspect. Clearly, the man was nervous.

"You know, Molly," Helene said, "I've never trusted that man. Something about him . . ." Her voice trailed off, and then she looked at Molly in surprise. "I wouldn't put murder past him. No, I wouldn't."

CHAPTER XXIV

Saturday night in the saloon district of Wolf Ridge was raucous and wild, like some bizarre rite of spring. Cowhands and railroaders fought, made up, and staggered from one saloon or gambling parlor to the next as though eager to lose their month's pay and loosen their teeth. The night was filled with clashing music from upright pianos, fiddles, and one brass band, along with shouts from the men and shrieks from women in dance halls and saloons.

Despite this unbridled chaos, Molly saw a certain propriety in force as she walked the boardwalks of this street lit by lamps flaring inside busy establishments. Gunplay and knife fights were quickly interrupted by a pair of burly deputies armed with sawed-off shotguns. But the many fistfights and the kick-and-claw wrestling matches in the street were allowed to progress to their bloody conclusions, and drunks of either sex were permitted to weave their foggy paths to a night of oblivion.

Molly had caught up with Buster Welch here after Asa Lemmon had beaten a hasty retreat to his suite in The Montanan. Now she watched from the opposite side of the street while Welch and several Bar S Bar cowhands lurched into the Wolf's Den, a crowded and smoky saloon where women stood just inside the bat-wing doors beckoning passersby to come in and sample the delights.

Molly's gaze went down the length of the boardwalk on which she stood, her attention caught by a figure down there. Shouldering his way past men crowding into a brightly lit dance hall, Sheriff Jenkins came toward her.

"What're you doing down here?" he asked when he reached her.

Something in his expression and tone of voice prompted Molly to say, "I've got a feeling you already know, sheriff."

"My deputies noticed you," he said. He studied her. "You're trailing Welch, ain't you?"

Molly nodded, looking at the lawman's scarred face cast in lamplight from the nearby dance hall. Music abruptly started up in there, followed by a chorus of enthusiastic shouts and rhythmic boot stomping on the plank floor.

Sheriff Jenkins spoke over the din: "You figure he's the one who gunned down

Brooks, is that it?"

"He's a suspect," Molly said.

Jenkins shook his head. "Welch has half a dozen cowhands who claim he was riding the range with them that day. I don't figure any way he could have been two places at once."

Molly acknowledged the point with a nod.

"Look, Miss Owens," Jenkins said, leaning closer to her, "you'd damn well better come clean with me. If you know anything, I want to hear it. Sam's going crazy in that cell. If he's innocent, I want him out of there — now."

"Sheriff, if I had the evidence to convict someone else," she said, "I'd turn it over to you."

"You must have something on Welch," he said, "or you wouldn't be trailing him. Now, I want to know what it is."

Molly knew that Jenkins would not be satisfied with a vague answer. She nodded and motioned for him to step away from the blaring noise of the dance hall. In the quiet shadows beyond a saloon next door she explained Buster Welch's role in her theory of the murder of Preston Brooks.

"Asa Lemmon," Jenkins whispered. "Damn, you just may be right about him.

He's a cold fish. You figure he had something to gain by Brooks' death?"

"I can't prove it," Molly said. "Not yet."

"Wouldn't surprise me a bit if Buster had some idea of taking over the Bar S Bar," Jenkins said. "Not one bit." He paused. "You say you're looking for proof. I wish to hell we could speed things up a bit."

"Maybe we can," Molly said.

"You mean there's something else you know that you haven't told me?" he said.

"No," Molly said, "but an idea just came to me. I'll need your help to make it work."

"What do I have to do?" Jenkins asked.

"Toss Buster Welch in jail," Molly said. "Can you find a reason to arrest him?"

"I reckon I could if I put my mind to it," Jenkins replied. "But what good will that do?"

"It may do two things," Molly said. "For one thing, you can make Buster think he's a prime suspect in the murder of Preston Brooks. You can lead him to believe that he was seen with Streeter's Arabian that day or that he was seen carrying the .44-40 hunting rifle."

"I see," Jenkins said. "Maybe we can crack his story. Then he'll name Lemmon."

Molly nodded. "I'll watch Lemmon. When he finds out Welch is in jail, he may do something foolish, something that will incriminate him."

"By god," Jenkins said, "it's worth a try. It sure as hell is."

Risky, too, Molly thought. If the plan failed, her investigation would be finished. And Sam Streeter's fate would be sealed.

Molly awakened early in the morning. She dressed and opened her door a crack. Moving the chair near the door, she sat down and began her vigil. When Lemmon left his suite, she'd trail him. Last night she had witnessed the arrest of Buster Welch, watching from across the street as the handcuffed foreman, protesting all the way, was hauled off to jail.

Lemmon slept late, not going downstairs for breakfast until after midmorning. Molly watched him from a back corner of the lobby and later followed at a distance as he walked to the NA&P depot. From a side window of the building Molly saw him talking to the telegrapher, a ticket agent, and two other railroad men lounging over a morning cigar.

Presently Sheriff Jenkins entered the building and joined the group. If Lemmon had not yet heard about Welch's arrest, Molly thought, he was hearing it now. A quarter of an hour later Jenkins left the depot, and Molly caught his eye.

"Figured you wouldn't be too far away," he said, meeting her around the corner of the depot. "Lemmon never even flinched when I mentioned the fact that Welch is cooling his heels in my jail."

"What about Buster?" Molly asked. "Did you get anything out of him last night?"

"Nope," Jenkins replied. "I questioned him drunk, and I questioned him sober. He denies knowing anything." The lawman shook his head. "I can't hold him much longer. Last night I pulled him in for public drunkenness, but he's stone sober now — and hopping mad."

"Can you hold him for the rest of the day?" Molly asked.

Jenkins nodded. Grim-faced, he was clearly worried.

Molly did not say so, but she was worried, too. Half an hour later she followed Asa Lemmon as he left the depot with a newspaper under his arm. He returned to The Montanan and climbed the stairs to his suite.

From her position inside the door of her room Molly spent the rest of the morning watching the hallway. Lemmon was obviously spending this Sunday in relaxation. He certainly did not behave like a murderer whose conspirator was in jail.

Shortly after noon Molly heard his door open and close, but did not see him come to the head of the stairs. She jumped to her feet. Grabbing her handbag, she hurried out. Lemmon had left the hotel by the fire exit.

Molly bounded down the back stairs and reached the alley in time to see Lemmon reach the rear entrance of the homestead locator office. She watched him go in, and hurried down there.

The back door was ajar. Molly drew her revolver as she edged toward it. She peered in, wondering now if she had overlooked incriminating documents that Lemmon had come here to destroy.

Molly pushed the door open a few more inches. She did not see Lemmon inside. An instant later a gun barrel punched into her back, and she realized she had been led into a trap.

"Drop that gun," Lemmon growled, "and get inside."

Molly complied and stepped into the doorway. Lemmon gave her a hard shove. She stumbled into the back room and lost her balance. She fell to the floor.

Rolling over, Molly saw Lemmon pick up her handbag. He pulled it open and plunged a hand inside, looking at the contents.

"Gun, keys, and a set of lock probes," he said, tossing the handbag aside. He leveled his small revolver at her. "I figured you were the only person in this cowtown who could go through a locked door without breaking it down. You've been through this office, and you've gone through my room. Just what the hell are you up to?"

Molly sat up. "I'm investigating the murder of Preston Brooks."

"And you think I had something to do with that?" he demanded. "By god, I ought to slap some sense into you."

"Where were you the day he was murdered?" Molly asked.

Lemmon replied with a curse. "Preston Brooks was a great man in this country. He had a dream for the West. You're crazy if you think I killed him."

"You still haven't answered my question," Molly said.

"I'm not going to, either," he said. "I don't answer to you. What I will do is press charges against you for breaking and entering."

"Good," Molly said. "Then you can explain everything to Sheriff Jenkins."

"I have nothing to hide," Lemmon said. "But I sure as hell ought to teach you a lesson, a good one that you won't soon forget."

Face red with anger, Lemmon went on, "Damned if I can figure you. Why are you trying so hard to spring Sam Streeter out of jail — especially after what he did to you?"

"I think he's innocent," Molly said.

"Innocent," Lemmon repeated. "Streeter should have been in jail a long time ago for harboring train robbers."

"That doesn't mean he should go to the gallows for a crime he didn't commit," Molly said.

"I don't care what happens to him," Lemmon said. He drew a breath. "You've been following me like a bloodhound. You've ransacked my room and my office. Now you're accusing me of murdering a man I respected." He drew his foot back and kicked her.

Molly doubled over and tried to block the blow. The toe of his shoe did not get past her elbows.

"Where were you that day?" Molly asked.

"Shut up," Lemmon said. "You just don't give up, do you? Maybe you are right. Maybe someone pinned the murder on Streeter. But you're sure as hell on the wrong trail. The suspect you ought to be going after is right under the nose of you and that thick-headed sheriff."

"If you're talking about Buster Welch —" Molly began.

"You'll find out who I'm talking about," Lemmon said, thrusting his handgun into his pocket. "In due time you'll find out, and we'll get this thing over with once and for all. Now, get out!"

CHAPTER XXV

When Molly went downstairs for breakfast Monday morning she was notified by the desk clerk that a telegraphed message awaited her at the depot. She left The Montanan immediately and hurried up there.

She received it at the telegrapher's window. Tearing open the envelope, she read through it in hopes of finding the answer to a question that had kept her awake last night. She was disappointed.

While this was not the report that had been occupying her mind, she was not particularly surprised by the contents. It was a background report on Asa Lemmon, and it was thorough. No evidence had been found that pointed to a motive for him to murder Preston Brooks.

Molly returned to the hotel dining room and ate breakfast. Looking out the window, she saw a man who looked vaguely familiar go into the county sheriff's office. Presently he came out with the sheriff, and they headed across the street for the front door of The Montanan.

Molly now recognized the clerk who worked in the homestead locator office.

His name was George, she remembered, and he was clearly distressed as he walked rapidly across Main Street, urging Jenkins to hurry.

Molly left a fresh cup of coffee and two pieces of buttered toast behind as she put money on the table and hurried out to the lobby. She saw Jenkins and the clerk near the top of the stairs.

She followed and caught up with the two men as they reached the door to Lemmon's suite. Jenkins acknowledged her presence with a terse nod while George knocked loudly.

"See, he doesn't answer," George said. "Sheriff, this isn't like him, not a bit like him —" He turned, surprised to see Molly standing beside the lawman.

"I'll get a passkey down at the desk," Jenkins said.

"I can open it," Molly said.

"Who are you?" George demanded in a frantic voice.

"Calm down," Jenkins said, "and stand aside. Let the lady do her work."

"What's going on —"

Before George could finish, Jenkins reached out and grasped his arm. He pulled the clerk away from the door.

Molly reached into her handbag and

brought out the lock probe she had used before. She inserted it into the keyhole and slowly drew it out. The lock released with a soft *click*. She turned the handle, and the door swung open.

The amazement that registered on George's face was quickly replaced by horror as he looked into the hotel suite. He uttered a small cry and turned away, collapsing against the doorjamb. Jenkins moved past him, and Molly followed.

Asa Lemmon lay face down across the bed, which was stained with his blood. Molly moved closer as Jenkins turned the body over. The mortal wound was a small hole in the center of Lemmon's chest.

Clenched in the dead man's hand was a small gun. As Jenkins pried the fingers away from the weapon, Molly recognized the .32-caliber revolver that Lemmon had pulled on her last night.

"Looks like we've got our killer," Jenkins said, straightening up. He turned to Molly. "Lemmon knew we were closing in on him, and he found a way out."

"Can we prove it?" Molly asked.

Jenkins shrugged. "Welch can."

"You still have him in custody?" Molly asked.

"I kept him all night," Jenkins replied,

"and figured to question him this morning. Now I'll tell him that Lemmon confessed. Maybe that'll open him up."

Molly left the sheriff to carry out his bluff with Buster Welch and looked for Helene. At the Wolcott house she learned that Helene had returned to the ranch yesterday. Molly rented a saddle horse and made a hard ride to the Bar S Bar.

Helene met Molly at the door of the ranch house. She seemed to have aged visibly since Molly had last seen her. Lines at the corners of her mouth had deepened, and she slumped at the shoulders as though burdened.

"Molly," Helene said in surprise. "What are you doing here? Is . . . is something wrong? Is Sam all right?"

"Your husband is all right," Molly said, "but Asa Lemmon isn't — as you well know."

"What on earth are you talking about?" Helene asked.

"You can drop the act," Molly said.

"Molly —" she began.

"You shot Asa Lemmon," Molly said. "You were his judge and jury, weren't you?"

Helene drew her lips into a fine line.

"I know you did it," Molly said. "And I know why."

Helene's mouth quivered, and her eyes filled with tears. She sobbed.

"Oh, Molly," she said through her tears, "I had to, don't you see? That man was a cold-blooded killer. My husband would have hanged for the murder he committed."

Helene wiped her eyes. "I went to his room in the hotel last night and confronted him. He didn't even bother to deny it, Molly. He laughed at me and waved that little gun in my face. Molly, he taunted me!"

Helene sobbed again, breathing raggedly while she spoke. "I don't know what happened exactly, but I lunged for him. I was going to scratch his eyes out, I guess, but my fingers closed around his gun. He fell back, pulling me with him. The gun went off, and he made a strange sound. I raised up. He was dead. Just like that, Molly, he was dead. I didn't know what to do. I was going to report it, but as I went out into the hallway I changed my mind. Molly, he deserved to die.

"I went back into his room and put the gun in his hand, then I left the hotel by the back stairs. No one saw me. That little gun didn't make enough noise to alert anyone. All I could think about then was coming home. I wanted to be here, waiting for my Sam."

She reached out and grasped Molly's hands. "Oh, Molly, don't you understand? Surely, you do . . . you of all people."

Molly looked on as the others crowded around Sheriff Jenkins. The lawman sat at his desk. Helene stood before him, her face drawn. Sam Streeter was beside her, hand-cuffed, and Alfred Wolcott stood nearby. On the other side of the desk Claus Eberhardt watched, his intense, birdlike eyes darting back and forth. They had all just listened to Helene's confession of murder.

Wolcott broke the silence with his deep, authoritative voice: "I want my client released, sheriff."

Claus Eberhardt moved a step closer. "This is a capital crime. Streeter cannot be released without a hearing." He cast a meaningful look at Jenkins. "Am I correct, sheriff?"

"Don't worry, Eberhardt," he replied, "the letter of the law will be followed around here. As soon as I can notify Judge Garret, you'll have your hearing. Right now he's out of town, in Helena, I think. I'll get a wire off to him that he's needed here."

Sheriff Jenkins stood. "In the meantime I'm gonna have to hold you, Sam. And you, Mrs. Streeter, I want you to stay with the Wolcotts." He turned to Alfred Wolcott. "As an officer of the court, I'm remanding her to your custody."

Wolcott replied with a nod. "All right, Sheriff."

Molly began to leave the office with the others, but was called aside by Jenkins. She waited while he returned Sam Streeter to his cell, and when the lawman came back they were alone in the office.

"You've got a way of striking out on your own without telling me what you plan to do," Jenkins said. "You left me to work on Welch while you went after a murderer."

"I wasn't positive Helene had shot Asa Lemmon until she confessed," Molly said. "If she had denied it, I'd have come back empty-handed."

"Well, I've got to hand it to you," Jenkins conceded a bit unhappily, "you made things happen in a hurry. You saw through this thing. I just figured Lemmon had committed suicide, and all I could think about was breaking Welch's story."

"Did you?" Molly asked.

Jenkins shook his head. "I did everything short of beating the truth out of him." He added, "At noon I had to let him go."

Molly moved toward the door.

"You think Mrs. Streeter's testimony will hold up in court?" Jenkins asked.

Molly stopped at the door and said, "I think Helene has confessed to a murder that will go unpunished."

"That's what I figure, too," Sheriff Jenkins said. "She picked a hell of a way to get her husband out of jail, didn't she?"

After leaving the county sheriff's office, Molly went directly to the train depot. At the telegrapher's window she sent an urgent message to Horace Fenton in New York. Then she went to Lillie's place.

CHAPTER XXVI

Three days later the Wolf Ridge Community Hall was jammed with onlookers from town and the outlying ranches and farms. As in a midweek holiday, the people had come for the hearing of Helene Streeter before Judge Garret.

Outside, the air of spring was still, with a glaring sun in a clear sky, and even though all windows and both doors in the meeting hall were wide open, the heat inside was nearly unbearable. Women waved paper fans in front of their faces, and men sat stoically with their straw hats on their laps, drops of sweat trickling down their white foreheads to their sunburned faces.

Molly had taken a chair on the aisle in the first row. She was behind the table where Helene sat beside her attorney, Alfred Wolcott. In the same row, three seats down from Molly, Sam Streeter sat beside Sheriff Jenkins. The rancher's thick wrists were shackled.

Across the aisle sat Lillie. The madam wore a long pink dress with puffed sleeves, and a large plumed hat. She sat still and stiff-necked, obviously uncomfortable to be there. Straight ahead of her at the other table before the bench sat Claus Eberhardt, his eyes darting about the room.

Molly looked around, too. Missing, she realized, was Judith Wolcott. Molly noticed that none of the other members of the Decency League she had seen parade through the saloon district after picketing Lillie's place were here, either.

The hum of whispers from the onlookers was silenced by the appearance of the black-robed Judge Garret. Taking his seat behind the makeshift bench, he banged the gavel once. He stated the purpose of the hearing and then called for testimony.

Molly listened as Sheriff Jenkins described the discovery of Asa Lemmon's body. While questioned by Claus Eberhardt, the bald lawman sat holding his Stetson in his hands, turning it slowly as he answered.

Next Helene took the stand. Molly heard scuffs of shoe leather and a whisper of heavy fabric as all the onlookers leaned forward in their chairs. They strained to hear the voice of this woman who had become such a hot topic of conversation in the last three days.

Helene began her confession in a sure and steady voice, but by the time she finished her voice was choked with emotion, and tears ran down her powdered cheeks. When she finished, a great sigh came from the audience, a spontaneous expression of sympathy for the woman.

"Is there any additional testimony to be given here today?" Judge Garret asked in a perfunctory tone. He raised his gavel, ready to end the hearing.

"I have testimony to enter into the record," Molly said, standing. All eyes turned to her, including Helene's. She turned in her chair and looked at Molly in surprise.

"Step forward and identify yourself," Judge Garret said.

Molly moved up between the two tables and faced the bench. "My name is Molly Owens. I am an operative for the Fenton Investigative Agency, and I've been involved in the investigation of this case, starting with the murder of Preston Brooks."

"I remember," the judge said, an eyebrow raised. "You were named by Sheriff Jenkins in his testimony. You were present when the body of Asa Lemmon was discovered, is that correct?"

"Yes, your honor," Molly said.

"And you wish to give testimony in this case?" he asked.

"I want to bring forward two witnesses —" Molly began.

"Your honor," Alfred Wolcott said, rising, "I object to this. Miss Owens is not an officer of the court and has no right to bring witnesses in here."

"This is highly irregular, Miss Owens," Judge Garret said.

"The witnesses will give information that is important to this case," Molly said. "And their testimony will shed new light on the murder of Preston Brooks."

"Your honor!" Wolcott exclaimed. "This isn't a trial —"

Claus Eberhardt, silent until now, leaped out of his chair. "I want to hear this testimony, your honor."

The judge struck the table top with his gavel. "I'm well aware that no one is on trial here, Mr. Wolcott. However, the task at hand is to gather as much evidence and testimony as possible. I will listen and decide if the new testimony is germane to these proceedings. Miss Owens, who is your first witness?"

"Miss Lillie Jones," Molly said.

A collective gasp came from the onlookers as Lillie stood and came forward. Judge Garret gaveled for silence and then swore Lillie in as a witness. The fat woman lowered herself into the chair beside the bench.

Molly asked, "How well did you know Preston Brooks?"

"Pretty well," Lillie replied. "Very well, I'd say. He generally came to my place for a drink when he was in town."

"Did he tell you about an intimate relationship he was having with a woman in Wolf Ridge?" Molly asked.

Lillie nodded. "Yeah, that's right. Pres was trying to break it off, and we talked about it quite a bit."

"Who was this woman?" Molly asked.

Lillie said matter-of-factly, "Helene Streeter."

The courtroom erupted. Alfred Wolcott shouted his objection, and all the onlookers exclaimed to each other in utter surprise. Judge Garret repeatedly hammered the table with his gavel until the room was silent.

"Another outburst like that," he said, "and I'll clear this courtroom. Take your seat, Mr. Wolcott." He turned to Molly. "Now, Miss Owens, what you have brought here is a witness who can only give hearsay testimony. I cannot allow such testimony to be entered on the record unless your witness was an actual witness to the relationship she described. Was she?"

"Yes, your honor," Molly replied.

"All right, let her describe what she saw," Judge Garret said, waving a hand at Alfred Wolcott who had again stood to make an objection.

Lillie said, "Well, I saw them together. Pres and Mrs. Streeter were in his private railcar one night. I was just leaving, and I looked back through a window in the door and saw her. They embraced, and that was all I saw."

Judge Garret asked, "And you never saw them together after that?"

"No, sir," Lillie said.

"All right," he said, "you may step down."

"Your honor," Wolcott said, standing. "Other than publicly embarrassing my client, I fail to see how the cause of justice has been furthered by slanderous testimony from a prostitute."

"Now, you listen here, buster," Lillie said, raising a fist at Wolcott.

Judge Garret again pounded the tabletop. Like a ship at sea, Lillie altered her course and returned to her chair.

"Miss Owens," the judge said, "just what bearing does that testimony have on this case?"

"My next witness will clarify that," Molly said.

"Your honor, please —" Wolcott began.

Claus Eberhardt again stood. "I want to hear the testimony, your honor."

Molly's gaze was caught by Helene. She stared at Molly with hatred.

"I'm going along with this a while longer," Judge Garret said. "But mind you, I must be quickly convinced that this last testimony is relevant to the case. Who is your second witness?"

Molly turned and gestured to a man who stood at the open front door. A Fenton operative, he wore a bowler hat and a dark suit. At Molly's signal, he nodded to someone outside.

John Copeland appeared in the doorway and came forward. Walking down the aisle at his side was a young woman wearing a sunbonnet.

Molly turned back to face the judge. "Celia Copeland, your honor."

CHAPTER XXVII

She pulled off her sunbonnet as she came down the aisle beside her father, a beautiful young woman wearing a mail-order suit with a pleated skirt that reached to the pointed toes of her high-button shoes. She held her head high, looking straight ahead while she walked toward Molly and the judge's bench. Her father stood back, looking after her.

The courtroom was silent now as Celia Coleman came forward alone and identified herself to Judge Garret. In a clear tone of voice she swore on a Bible to tell the whole truth, and then took the stand.

Molly smiled at her, glad that Celia had not lost her resolve. She had arrived by train only yesterday, and Molly had spent much of the evening with her and her parents.

"You are carrying Preston Brooks' child, aren't you?" Molly asked.

"Yes," Celia replied softly.

"Please tell the judge about your relationship with Preston Brooks," Molly said.

"We were to be married," Celia said.

"And why weren't you?" Molly asked.

"Because of her," Celia replied.

"Who?" Molly asked.

"Mrs. Streeter," Celia said.

"Your honor, I think this has gone far enough," Alfred Wolcott said.

"I strongly disagree, your honor," Claus Eberhardt countered.

"Gentlemen, take your seats," Judge Garret said. He turned his gaze back to Celia Copeland. "Please go on."

"Well," Celia said, "Pres told me that he and Mrs. Streeter were lovers before he met me. He said Mrs. Streeter had begged him to take her out of Montana —"

An anguished cry filled the courtroom. Molly turned to see Sam Streeter, his mouth twisted open, stretch his shackled arms toward his wife. Helene covered her face with her hands.

"Your honor, this is hearsay, slanderous hearsay!" Wolcott bellowed.

Judge Garret nodded agreement. "The testimony is hearsay, Miss Owens. I must ask you not to pursue this line of questioning. If the defendant cannot speak from her own experience, then I'll have to call an end to these proceedings."

"Celia's testimony can be corroborated," Molly said.

"You don't understand," the judge said. "Without Preston Brooks, no one can corroborate the testimony except Mrs. Streeter. Such questioning can only take place at a trial. And Mrs. Streeter is not on trial here."

"Your honor," Molly said, "I believe this testimony can be corroborated by someone else."

"Who?" he asked.

"Sam Streeter," Molly replied. She turned to face the rancher as all eyes went to him.

Streeter stood, seemingly unaware of anyone but his wife. He stared at her back, hands out in front of him in a pleading gesture.

"My god, Helene," he said hoarsely, "how could you . . . why . . . why?"

Helene suddenly banged her hands down on the table. She whirled to face him. "Sam, you abandoned me a long time ago! When I couldn't give you what you wanted most, a child, you abandoned me."

She drew a deep breath, the years of stored anger boiling over. "You devoted your life to that ranch, to your precious bulls and stallions. They reproduced, didn't they? Is that why you loved them so much?"

Helene shook away Wolcott's hand when he reached out to her. "You haven't loved me for years," she went on. "You used me like a servant, used me in the worst way that a man can use a woman."

Sam Streeter slowly shook his head. "Brooks . . . you used him . . . to get back at me." He spoke as though dazed.

"You'll never understand what I felt for him," she said. "Pres was a man, a real man —"

"Your honor!" Wolcott interrupted. "This court has degenerated into a forum for my client's humiliation! I demand that it cease!"

Molly faced the judge as he spoke. "Miss Owens, you have misled me. We're not here to listen to sordid details of private lives." He raised his gavel, ready to end the hearing.

"But, your honor," Molly said, "don't you see? Sam Streeter knows the truth now. Ask him."

"The truth?" Judge Garret said, mystified.

"Helene murdered Preston Brooks," Molly said, turning to her.

A hush swept over the courtroom. Judge Garret stared, amazed, his gavel poised in midair. The silence was at last broken by Sam Streeter.

"Helene . . . why? Why?"

Molly said, "You couldn't have Preston Brooks, and you no longer wanted your husband. Isn't that right, Helene?"

Helene whirled, facing Molly. "You lousy bitch!"

"Last year you showed your anger by shooting two Percheron horses, didn't you?" Molly asked. "You saw what that did to your husband, so this year you used the same idea to get him away from the ranch. And then you took his gun and his horse, and you rode to the spot where you knew you'd find Preston Brooks. You're a good shot, Helene. One bullet was all it took, because you knew how to use your husband's hunting rifle from the times you hunted deer and elk."

In the hushed silence of the meeting hall, Molly went on, "You rode that lame Arabian back to the ridge, where you watched to make sure no one followed. Then you went home, after leaving two clues behind — the cigarillo from your husband's ashtray and the shell casing from his rifle. If the suspicion of guilt wasn't enough, the circumstantial evidence would convict him. That was your plan, wasn't it?"

Helene softly cursed her.

"After your husband was arrested," Molly said, "you gave the greatest performance of your life, didn't you? You had to use all of your acting skills when you became the distraught wife valiantly defending your husband. All the while you wanted to see him hang."

A sob wracked Helene. Her defiant pose broke, and her shoulders shook as she bowed her head, crying.

"Your honor," Wolcott pleaded.

Judge Garret banged the gavel on the table. "I want this courtroom cleared. The hearing will resume in my chambers." He stood and strode away from the bench, his black robe billowing out behind him.

"Like I said, Miss Owens, you've got a way of keeping things to yourself. When did you know she was guilty?"

Molly stood with Sheriff Jenkins on the boardwalk in front of his office. Her handbag was over her shoulder and her packed valise at her feet. A passenger train was pulling into the depot, and now Molly heard the engine's bell ringing.

"When we found Asa Lemmon's body," Molly said, "Welch was in jail. That was when I realized Helene was the overlooked suspect in the case. She had the opportunity, more than anyone else. I remembered that every time Preston Brooks was in Wolf

Ridge, she was here, too. Lemmon must have known they were having an affair. That was what led him to her."

"And to his death," Jenkins added. "In her confession, she said Lemmon tried to blackmail her. He had some idea about getting some of the money from the sale of the Bar S Bar once Sam was convicted." He paused. "She was quite an actress, like you said in court. She fooled all of us — you, too."

Molly nodded. "I couldn't prove my theory about her until I got the report on Celia Copeland. After that, it was a matter of convincing her to return to Wolf Ridge. And convincing Lillie that she had to testify."

"She told me that she owed it to Brooks," Jenkins said, "even though it went against her nature to talk about it."

"She has her own sense of ethics, doesn't she?" Molly said.

"Don't tell that to the Decency League," Jenkins said, with half a grin. He paused. "I don't reckon we'll ever know if Brooks would have married Celia, will we?"

"I know she believes he intended to," Molly said. "That's good enough for me."

"The Copelands have decided to stay in Wolf Ridge," Jenkins said. "John told me they had a long talk after the hearing and decided they weren't going to be run out of town by gossip."

"I'm happy to hear that," Molly said. She paused. "How's Sam Streeter?"

"Haven't seen him," Jenkins said. "Once I took the shackles off, he headed straight for his ranch and hasn't come back to town since. I do know that he fired Buster Welch. Welch came through town on his way to Wyoming. He was pretty mad that I kept him locked up like I did. Couldn't seem to understand that if he'd been loose, he'd have been accused of killing Asa Lemmon."

"That's right," Molly said.

"You know, I figured Sam ought to thank you for springing him out of my jail," Jenkins said, "but he wouldn't hear of it. I think he'll regret that one day."

"Maybe," Molly said. "But if I gave him his freedom, I took something away from him, too."

The train whistle sounded three short blasts. Molly shook hands with the lawman and bid him goodbye. She picked up her valise.

"Well, so long," Jenkins said. "You oughta come back this way sometime. The Copelands think the world of you. So does

Lillie. Matter of fact, so do I. I could use a deputy like you."

Molly smiled. "I may take you up on that one day, sheriff."

She left the lawman there and walked toward the depot, hearing the sounds of the steam engine. She would never again hear a train without memories of Preston Brooks coming to mind.

The right man. In Pres she'd had another glimpse of him. He was a man of action who was guided by a vision of the future. He was a complex man, and a good one.

When she had recounted her investigation to Sheriff Jenkins, she'd omitted an important detail, one that she would never be able to explain to anyone. The sound of a distant train whistle when she had stood face to face with Asa Lemmon had changed the course of her investigation. It had come to her like a voice from the grave. That sad voice had pointed the way.

The employees of Thorndike Press hope you have enjoyed this Large Print book. All our Large Print titles are designed for easy reading, and all our books are made to last. Other Thorndike Press Large Print books are available at your library, through selected bookstores, or directly from us.

For information about titles, please call:

(800) 223-1244
(800) 223-6121

To share your comments, please write:

Publisher
Thorndike Press
P.O. Box 159
Thorndike, Maine 04986

W